DANCING WITH FATE

by

Hywela Lyn

To Rob
with very
best wishes
from

Hywela Lyn

Dancing with Fate

ISBN: 978-1463500559

Cover Art by Miss Mae

Dedication

Dedicated to the memory of my own golden horse, Sally, who was the inspiration for Sal. Also in memory of Flikka, Star, Mr Fifty, and the dogs, Hans, Blaze, Bonnie and Bob, who I like to imagine playing together in their own Elysian fields.

With grateful thanks to my husband Dave for all his support and to my crit partner, the talented author Miss Mae, for all her help, encouragement and support in this story, as well as my other works. And for the beautiful cover she created for this edition.

Dancing with Fate is a work of fiction. Though some actual towns, cities, and locations may be mentioned, they are used in a fictitious manner and the events and occurrences were invented in the mind and imagination of the author. Any similarities of characters or names used within to any person past, present, or future is coincidental.

Contact information:
Hywelalyn@hywelalyn.co.uk.

Publishing History
First Wild Rose Press Faery Rose Edition, 2008

Other Books by Hywela Lyn

STARQUEST

CHILDREN OF THE MIST

More information about these and future books can be found at her website:

http://www.hywelalyn.co.uk

A taste of some of the Reviews for 'Dancing With Fate':

"Hywela Lyn is a skillful storyteller. I'm impressed by not only how her descriptions are rich, vibrant, and flowing, but how she weaves the qualities of courage, honor and loyalty into the question of how much a woman-mortal or not-will sacrifice to save the life of the man she loves. By the time you finish this book, you'll never look at the legend of Merlin, or the phrase 'dancing with fate' the same way again!"

~Miss Mae, Author of the best selling "See No Evil, My Pretty Lady etc.

"… For me, Greek mythology can be a bit hard to read. I do not know much about it, so it can be hard to follow. However, Ms. Lyn did such a fantastic job of describing each character that I never knew I could enjoy Greek myths quite so much. I wholeheartedly recommend this book, filled with vivid landscapes, Greek myths, and some of the strongest characters I have read in a while."

~Amaranth, Long And Short Reviews
- *Five Hearts*

In the valley so green, in the sunlight of morn,

The muse of the dance strays thoughtful and slow:

The flowers of spring her bright hair adorn,

But the wind through the trees sighs, laden with woe.

She looks o'er the mountains, heart filled with emotion,

And watches the Teifi to the great ocean flow.

"Cymru, poor Cymru," are the words softly spoken.

"Your music's forgotten, you live by the bow."

Chapter 1

Mount Olympus—the distant past

The last notes of the choir died away and the nine beautiful sisters made the slightest of curtsies to their leader. Apollo smiled in approval and the marble hall, with its gleaming pillars of white and gold, glowed in his radiance. When they turned to leave, he called to the one who played the lyre.

"Terpsichore—I would have a word with you." The lovely dark haired muse turned and glided back to where the god of light sat in splendor. He held his tripod in one hand and his bow hung over his shoulder. His own lyre or *kithara* lay on his knee. The brightness that emanated from him was such it almost dazzled even a muse such as herself. However, she met the brilliance of his eyes with pride, and lost none of her self-confidence.

Clasping her delicately carved instrument, she stood before him and nodded a polite greeting to his raven perched nearby. She inclined her head to one side, a question in her eyes. "You wish to speak with me my brother?"

"First, I would have you dance for me. You know how I love to see you dance."

Even if he had not been the Musagetes, leader of all the Muses, and her half brother, Terpsichore could still not have declined to grant his request. Golden hair, curling down nearly to his shoulders, framed his dazzling, almost frighteningly handsome features, crowned with a wreath of laurel leaves. His eyes, velvet brown in some lights, glittering gold in others, had a mesmerizing quality. His masculine physique was sheer perfection. Little wonder every goddess he looked upon with desire, instantly yielded to him, even without the assistance of Dionysus' enchanted wine.

Apollo nodded to her to begin. Raising her arms above her head, like a bird flexing its wings, Terpsichore drew music from her lyre with the plectrum. The notes rose and surrounded her like a magical veil of sound. Languidly, she moved in time to the music, allowing the silken folds of her long white garment to flow around her like soft ripples in a becalmed sea. She swiveled her hips faster. Bending backward, her body curved in a graceful arc, she placed the lyre against a pillar entwined with vines of gold, in a fluid movement that was part of her dance. With a toss of her head, she swung her long hair, braided with flowers and ribbons, over one shoulder. Her hands and arms moved with the grace of a gentle breeze bending the grass, as she accompanied herself with her own voice.

As always when she danced, Terpsichore lost herself in the rhythm. She hardly noticed when Apollo picked up his kithara and accompanied her singing. Her bare feet felt as though they no longer touched the ground as they performed the complex sequence of steps in time to her song and the swirling of her hips. It almost seemed as if time stood still and there was nothing but the magick of her dance.

Faster and faster she whirled, euphoric with the delight of doing what she loved best before someone who showed true appreciation. Then once more she slowed the rhythm and the dance became languorous, eminently sensual.

The remnants of her song faded and lingered for a moment in the crystal air. Terpsichore spread her arms in abeyance, then clasped her fingers in front of her, and stood for a moment in silence. Apollo lowered his instrument and clapped his hands, smiling and indicating she should sit beside him. She bent to retrieve her lyre, before seating herself and gazed at him, trying to hide her curiosity. "You wish something further of me, brother?"

For a long moment, Apollo seemed deep in thought and did not answer.

"Do you remember a land of mortals—a small country known as Cymru, the brotherhood, erstwhile called Cambria, or Wales as some would have it? You may recall the folk who inhabit it, who call themselves the Keltoi?"

The Celts. How could she forget them?

"I do. They were a fierce and noble race, with much knowledge of the powers of nature and the hidden arts. They respected the faeries and mages of their land. She smiled at the memory. "I inspired them with music and dancing which they embraced readily. I believe in times to come they will be famed for their love of melody, and the grace with which they express it in their singing and their dance."

A slight crease appeared on Apollo's brow, normally as smooth and clear as the polished black marble of the great throne of Zeus. "Only if you return to impart these skills once more; much has been lost in their skirmishes and fighting to protect their land. A great melancholy has come upon them. I need you to return and inspire them to dance again."

Terpsichore breathed a soft sigh that echoed through the hall like the singing of the breeze in summer leaves. "My lord—Apollo—I had not thought to return to the lands of mortals—not for a few hundred years, anyway. Is it truly necessary?"

Apollo's expression grew severe. A small frown played above his eyes and his face darkened slightly, like the sun going behind a cloud.

"Indeed it is, Terpsichore. As the Muse of Dance, it is your duty."

Terpsichore swallowed the sharp retort that rose in her throat. Duty indeed, how dare he suggest she was neglectful of her duty? He might be the magnificent, all-powerful Apollo, but she would not be patronized.

"My lord, have I not already done my duty? Did I not travel to every corner of the world and inspire men and women to dance and rejoice? Have I not made the journey whenever a mortal has been in need of my gift of inspiration, and gladdened the hearts of mankind? Can I be blamed if some prefer to fight and wage war and then forget the joys of living?"

Apollo's countenance grew even grimmer. "So many questions. No, 'tis not your doing—but would you refuse the task?"

Terpsichore sighed and shook her head. "Of course not. You know well that neither I nor my sister muses may deny our vocation. The need to inspire cannot be ignored."

Apollo curved his lips in a smile once more, and light radiated from his face, illuminating the shadows around him. "It is well; you will need to use subtlety, though. Times have changed since you were last there. It would be better for you to take the form of a mortal."

"What—give up my immortality?"

"No, not give it up. I doubt Zeus would allow that, nor would you want it from the expression on your face. Zeus and I have discussed the matter and feel you should pretend to be mortal for a while. Mingle with the people, bestow on them the enthusiasm to dance again." He paused. "Of course you will not be able to use any of your powers..." She drew in her breath, unable to hide her dismay. That could present a problem. She was not used to being without her magick.

Apollo seemed to read her thoughts. "At least," he went on, "not before mortals, or in a way it could be discerned. You must not allow your inner psyche to glow when you are among them. Know also, that your powers may wane and you may not be able to get inside their minds or use the gift of foretelling." He looked even more

5

serious. "If you have a problem, I may not be able to help you."

Oh wonderful - Although my being allowed some freedom might not be a bad thing. She gave him a knowing smile. "I suppose I'll manage. I may need to act the helpless female, but in reality I have a few tricks that may serve me well."

Apollo frowned again. "Take care not to get careless and reveal who you really are. The men of Cymru may not be as awestruck by a goddess as they once were. It could be risky. You would not want to be branded as a witch or an enchantress."

"You think I may be in danger?"

Apollo's frown deepened and his face registered concern. "No, sweet Terpsichore, I would not send you if I thought you might come to harm." He paused. "You will need a name to be known by." He thought for a moment. "Cora. You will go by the name of Cora, a name like enough to those of the common people."

Terpsichore nodded. She liked the sound of it, and it carried enough of her true name not to sound alien to her.

"Now go, prepare yourself, spend time in the Halls of Learning and familiarize yourself with the changes that have occurred since you last visited the land of Wales. Then bid your dear sisters farewell, before you take your leave of your mother and myself. Zeus will facilitate your departure and instruct the Horai to allow you passage through the gates of Olympus."

Terpsichore turned and clutched her lyre to her.

"I am to leave soon?"

"Why not? There is no reason to delay."

"No, of course not." A sudden thought struck her. "If I have to act as a mortal, how will I travel? Wales may not be a large country, but it is mountainous and, as I recall, not the easiest of terrain. It might be difficult to dance if I am footsore." A vision flashed into her mind of a beautiful winged horse, the color of the snow of the highest peak of Olympus. "Perhaps, I could have Pegasus?" she asked hopefully, although truly she knew the answer before he gave it. She always enjoyed riding Pegasus on the rare occasions her father felt disposed to allow it.

Apollo's eyes darkened for a moment, then the corners of his mouth turned up and he smiled once more. "A winged horse might give away the fact that you are not mortal, don't you think? Also, Zeus might be unwilling to loan his favorite steed for that length of time, even to one of his beloved daughters. Worry not. Take care to materialize outside settlements so as not to be observed by mortals. Should you need it, an appropriate means of transport will be arranged and you will not be disappointed."

A wave of his hand indicated the discussion was closed. With a little sigh, Terpsichore left her seat by his throne. When would she see the magnificent Olympus, her home, again? She would miss it. There again, now she'd had time to think upon it, she might even enjoy the task Apollo and her father had set her.

What was Apollo keeping hidden though? She could always tell when he was holding something back. What had he not told her? Still, he would surely have her best interests at heart.

No doubt, he would reveal it when he judged the time to be right.

She left the Great Hall through one of the rear doors. Was it her imagination or did she hear the sound of footsteps, as if someone scurried away down a side corridor? She glanced around and narrowed her eyes as she saw what looked like a tall figure slip into the shadows, but she could not be sure. It might just be a trick of the light. Had she imagined the dark form, the glint of torchlight on metal, gold or perhaps brass? Could someone have been eavesdropping on her conversation with Apollo? She hurried on silent feet to where she saw the figure disappear, but there was nothing. Nothing except a prickling at the back of her neck and the uncomfortable feeling she had not been mistaken.

Chapter 2

Ceredigion, Wales, 460 AD

The song of the Horai, the sisters who guarded the cloud gate of Olympus, still rang in Terpsichore's ears. The chill moisture of the clouds caressed her cheek. Surrounded by damp softness, she inhaled the aroma of mountain winds and sea salt, forest blossoms and moist leaves, and a wealth of other scents. When she touched the ground, the grass beneath her feet felt soft and cool, still damp with dew, the tears of the goddess, Eos. Why Eos wept every morning was a mystery; everyone knew she loved riding across the heavens in her chariot, drawn by her beloved horses, Lampos and Phaithon. Perhaps they were tears of joy for the new day.

Terpsichore gazed up to see Helios, Eos's brother, with his own team of horses: Bronte—Thunder, Steroes—Dazzling, Phlegon—Flaming and Pyrroes—Red-haired. They sped across the early morning sky and illuminated the clouds with hues of soft gold, silver and ochre. Eos opened the gates of the heavens for him at dawn, and traces of her rosy path remained, adding to the splendor of the morn.

All around her, bluebells carpeted the ground. Behind her rose a vast cliff, a waterfall spilling down its rocky face to combine with a deep pool below. Blossoms of every hue grew in mossy clefts and on the edge of the pool. Bordering the mountains a vast forest of oak and elm swept its branches skyward and splashes of gold showed where the early buds of gorse were coming into bloom. Even above the roar of the water, birdsong filled the air, and the scent of damp earth mingled with that of flowers. This land was as beautiful as when she visited it last.

Although drawn to the fall, as she always was to water, Terpsichore pushed any ideas of enjoying herself in its coolness to the back of her mind. She was here for a purpose, Apollo did not send her here to admire the scenery or partake of its offerings.

She glanced at her flowing *chiton*, girdled and reaching her feet. That would have to go, and so would the beautiful long *himation* draped over her shoulder. A sweep of her hands down her body and a Celtic *léine,* a long tunic of linen, replaced the chiton. A woollen *brat,* a shawl, fringed and colorfully stitched and decorated wrapped itself around her shoulders and covered her hair. She looked down at her toes. She preferred to go barefoot, or with light sandals, but the soft, damp grassland required something more substantial. In an instant, soft leather encased her feet.

She glanced southward, to where the nearest settlement lay. Soon it would be fully light. She must appear just outside the village without anyone seeing her materialize. Minutes later, she stood in the shadows. The small settlement was already awake and busy going about the routine of daily life. Women walked to the well to draw water and their children ran around or clutched at their mothers' hems. Men harnessed their animals, and some laid out wares on display. The noise of hammer against iron echoed back from the forge. The village was waking and preparing for the day.

There was something not right, though. A sense of melancholy pervaded. No one smiled, or laughed, or sang. They seemed to have forgotten how. She stepped into the open. Time to accomplish her task, and then she could return home.

~*~

Seven weeks later

Myrddin glanced around; unable to shake off the feeling he was not alone. Far above the outstretched arms of the nearby forest, beneath the slate cliff, a red kite hovered, its haunting cry sounding eerie and forlorn. He raised his arm in greeting. *"Good afternoon, my friend, would that I could join you."*

Mist drifted across the valley and the rays of the afternoon sun stained the sky in vivid shades of vermilion and orange. A doe, her fawn at her heels, touched his hand with her nose and a family of squirrels played around his feet. He moved forward slowly, gathering twigs for his fire pit, and glanced around every few moments. He must have imagined it, this sense of someone nearby. No sound disturbed the silence except the twittering of the birds, and the buzzing of tiny insects.

He turned to the doe. *"Time to take your baby home now, little one. You too, squirrels."* The doe gave him one last affectionate nuzzle, then trotted into the forest, and the squirrels scampered up a nearby oak.

Myrddin walked over to his horse, a sturdy beast, black as a starless, moonless night; its long mane fell in waves, nearly to its knees. Surely, Harri would know if a stranger was nearby, and would have warned him? The handsome horse snorted, nodding his head, and pawed the ground.

"Do you sense danger—has someone followed us?"

The horse merely gazed at him, with large, dark brown eyes.

"Well, you're don't seem worried, but I suppose you're hungry," he said aloud. "Then we'd better both have something to eat. This will be a good place to camp for the night. I think I must be in need of food and rest, myself, for I seem to be imagining things."

Myrddin put down his bundle of twigs and slipped a halter over the animal's head. He led him into the clearing where lush grass grew green and tender, before turning him loose. Returning to his fire, he checked it was not burning too fiercely and then rummaged under a small crop of rocks. His saddle and meager possessions lay in a hollow. He removed a tightly woven bag, from which he produced two fat trout. He made short work of preparing and gutting them. Next, he looked around for some large, flat leaves. Before long, he had the two fish tightly wrapped into a neat package, which he laid on the glowing embers. Then he carefully added the twigs to build the fire over them.

When he was sure the trout would cook through without burning, he removed his bow and quiver from his saddle pommel. The feeling he was not alone still troubled him. While his supper cooked, it would not do any harm to take a look around. He followed the stream that flowed through the little clearing. The area was new to him and he proceeded with some caution. Myrddin loved and respected all the creatures of the forests and mountains; he knew their ways and feared none of them. Likewise, no terrain, however difficult, caused him concern. Nothing in nature held any fears for him; people posed far more danger. There was someone close, a stranger. What were they doing here in the wilderness? Perhaps one of Madog's men lay in wait.

He had not walked far when he heard the sound of rushing water. Rounding the rocky promontory, he came upon a vast wall of water spilling down the cliff, feeding a deep pool of sparkling water below.

It was not that, however, which made him stop and stare in amazement.

~*~

How long had it been since she was last in this place? On Olympus, time meant little to a god, but in the land of mortals it was different. Terpsichore took a deep breath of the fresh mountain air and looked around. The grass seemed a little greener, the leaves on the trees darker, thicker. The season was drawing on toward summer. She studied the sky, the color of the bluebells which had carpeted the clearing when she first arrived, now replaced by blossoms of many different hues. A few wisps of cloud drifted lazily across and the air shimmered, warm and still.

Terpsichore was content. She'd travelled the length of Cymru and inspired men and women to dance again. Whenever she came across a receptive individual, she'd given her gift and they in turn encouraged others to dance. The shadows of war had lifted for a while, and once more, the land was filled with music and the delight of movement. She'd finished her task. Of course, the time would come when Cymru would again need to rise up against her oppressors and the hills would echo with the sound of fighting. Wales, land of song, would once more know sorrow. However, Terpsichore had chosen those she inspired with care. The music of Wales would not die again. This time, they would not let her down. The joy of the dance would remain whatever befell these people. Her mission completed, she could return to Olympus.

The sound of the waterfall behind her caught her attention. Oh, how she missed the spring of Hippocrene, created when Pegasus struck the rock of the Helicon Mountain with his hoof and the crystal water poured forth. Beautiful as this country was, it would be good to be home. She turned and gazed at the water tumbling down the mountainside in a frenzy of white froth, the spray catching the rays cast by Helios, making rainbows dance in the clear air. The water called to her—she was, after all, like her sisters, a water nymph. She longed to immerse herself in its cooling spray, to be as one with the living water.

"What harm can it do? Cleanse yourself—rid your body of the dust of Earth before returning to Olympus. "

The voice in her mind was all too familiar. *"Dionysus! What are you doing here? Get out of my mind"*

"Certainly, dear sister, would you prefer me to materialize in all my glory?"

Before she could answer, he appeared, seated upon a rock, his ever-present maenads fawning at his feet.

He held out a goblet of wine. "You seem in poor spirits, sister. Have a drink; it will put you in a better humor."

"My humor's fine, Dionysus. I'm about to go home. I don't need any of your wine." She turned her head away from the sight of the maenads drunkenly running their hands over his body.

All at once, the purity of the day seemed tainted. How had he found her? Was it he who had eavesdropped upon her conversation with Apollo? She sighed. Somehow, she did not think so. Dionysus in his state of permanent intoxication could hardly have moved so stealthily, nor concealed his retinue of women followers.

Dionysus hiccupped loudly, causing the vines around his neck to bounce and rustle.

Again, he held out the goblet of wine. "Oh, we are 'Miss Prim and Proper' today, aren't we? Go on, lighten up, take a sip, it won't hurt you." He learned toward her, his handsome, if somewhat effeminate features wearing an innocent expression that belied the glint in his blue eyes. "After all, you wouldn't want to upset your brother, would you?"

Terpsichore refrained from commenting that he was, in fact, only one of her many half-brothers. She pursed her lips, reached for the goblet and took a small sip, before handing it back. It did not do to offend the god. She recalled that despite his affable manner, he had a dark side and it was better not rub him up the wrong way. "Thank you. Now, I really must be leaving."

His smile was more of a smirk. "All right, I can take a hint. If I were you, I'd have a good long soak in that pool before you go. Go on, you know you want to."

He lurched unsteadily to his feet, causing one of his Maenads to loose her hold on him, and fall over, giggling. He grabbed her arm and moments later they all disappeared like mist in the heat of a summer's day.

To Hades with her demented half-brother. She pursed her lips. The more she thought about it, the more the allure of the water drew her to it. She should never have taken that wine—not even a sip. Who knew what enchantment he'd put in it?

She shrugged. What was she thinking? She was her own goddess, wasn't she? If she wanted to bathe, she would. She certainly didn't need any charmed wine to make her decisions for her. In an instant, her Celtic clothing melted away.

She laid her lyre against a friendly tree trunk and ran beneath the curtain of water cascading over the cliff face. She stood, waist deep in the shallows of the pool and let the water rush over her. The cold crystal clear liquid invigorated her. She felt the life force of the spring flow around and through her, the molecules that composed it, the tiny life forms unseen. This was her element and she rejoiced in it.

She went deeper and swam for a while, enjoying the freedom of movement in the water, playing with the little minnows that darted here and there. At last, she stepped out onto the grass that fringed the pool and looked skyward. How long had she been bathing? Helios was already on his homeward journey, although his light still warmed the air and he had not yet painted the sky in its twilight hues.

Shaking her arms free of the silvery drops of water, the muse then squeezed the wetness from her long hair, of which she was inordinately proud. Of all her womanly attributes, she loved her hair the best. It was so fine and silky; it took hardly any time to dry. She spread her arms and let the warm air vanquish the last of the moisture from her skin. Oh, this land was fair! She raised her arm in salute to Helios, knowing he could see whatever his warmth touched.

Terpsichore twirled around on tiptoe, bending back her head and taking in the craggy mountaintops, the trees full-leafed and swaying slightly in the warm breeze. On an impulse, she began to dance. She conjured up a silky himation between her fingers and swirled it above her head as she moved to the accompaniment of her own voice. So involved was she in her dancing she failed to realize she was no longer alone.

~*~

She was the loveliest woman Myrddin had ever seen. Spellbound, he watched her step from the falls. He should have turned away but he found it impossible not to watch her as she dried herself. When she started to dance, he was captivated by her grace and the eloquence of her movements. She seemed unconcerned about her nakedness. Not that she had anything to be ashamed of; such exquisite beauty should not be covered. Long, dark red-brown hair fell like a veil of silk to below her knees. Her skin was smooth and flawless; her breasts firm and high, full but not heavy, above a tiny waist.

Her rounded hips undulated sensuously in time to her singing, while her upper body remained perfectly still, apart from the expressive movements of her arms. Her legs were slim and very long and she moved on tiptoe, her small feet scarcely seeming to touch the ground. Between her fingers, she held a long piece of silky material, which she swirled around her, until it seemed almost like a living thing.

Myrddin watched, enthralled. He'd never known anyone to dance as she did. The way she swiveled her hips had him mesmerized. Her voice was soft and clear, with a haunting quality. It reminded him of the musical bells of *Maes Gwyddno*, the civilization that now lay drowned beneath the sea. At times of danger, if one listened hard enough, one could hear the bells ringing from beneath the waves. Moreover, it may have been a trick of the light, but she seemed to radiate a soft glow, pure and shimmering. He shook his head in disbelief. He must be imagining it. He'd eaten nothing since dawn, this was surely a vision brought on by weakness from hunger.

Myrddin crept closer and a twig cracked underfoot. Before he could take cover, the beautiful dancer stood motionless. Her eyes, green as the depths of the ocean, looked directly into his.

Chapter 3

Terpsichore stared at the stranger. She'd been too engrossed in her dance to notice she was no longer alone. With a swift movement of her hand, she clothed herself in the léine and brat. Her nakedness did not trouble her, she was well aware of the perfection of her body. However, she remembered Apollo's warning about not drawing attention to herself.

How long had he stood watching her? Should she risk using her sorcery to make him forget?

One look at his face, however and all such thoughts flew from her mind. A strong jaw, pale complexion, firm mouth and eyes as blue and gentle as the Aegean Sea on a sunny day, set her heart beating with unexpected desire. Golden hair, rivaling that of

Apollo himself, touched his broad shoulders. He was young, but his face held the assurance of a man much older. He wore a reddish brown inar or tunic, fastened with a leather belt, and long truis clad his legs. Common soldiers' garb—but she felt sure he was no common soldier. Although he had the bearing of a warrior, she suspected he might be a chieftain or nobleman. His brat, draped over one shoulder, was fringed and decorated in rich purple and gold—the mark of someone of high standing and nobility, not something an ordinary soldier would wear.

Very tall, and slender, he had strength about him. The man reminded her of a tree that would bend in a storm but not break. That was not all. His aura told her he was, indeed, no ordinary man. Never had she seen a mortal man so striking. He might not be as devastatingly handsome as some, perhaps, but beautiful none the less. His face was, oh, so pleasing to look upon, despite the unusual paleness of his skin. Not an unhealthy palor, but not tanned as one might expect, although it went well with his blond hair. There was unique character there, something that set him apart from his fellow men and went deeper than looks. She wanted to gaze at him forever.

She would have touched his mind with her own but at that moment, he spoke; the rich timbre of his voice sending shivers through her soul.

"Forgive me, lady, I had no wish to intrude, or to startle you."

"Worry not, stranger. You did not startle me. I am not frightened so easily."

"No, that much is apparent."

Was he laughing at her? His tone was polite, but his eyes held a sparkle that threatened to make her forget she was a goddess.

She pulled her brat closer around her. What brings you here stranger, so far away from any township?"

He smiled. "I was about to ask the same of you. And my name's not 'Stranger', it's Myrddin. Myrddin Ab Morfryn."

"You may call me, Cora."

He raised a quizzical eyebrow. "And do you mind if I ask where you are travelling to—alone?"

"I am returning home—to my family."

"There are dangers for a young woman alone—is your home far? Perhaps we could ride together. Two travelling together are safer than one."

The idea of spending time with this intriguing stranger was tempting. But Apollo and her sisters were surely waiting for her return. She shook her head. "No , thank you for your concern, but I can defend myself if need be." She indicated the knife tucked in her belt. Something made her glance toward the tree where she'd left her lyre. Beside the instrument stood a bow and quiver—they had not been there before she entered the falls. It seemed Apollo was trying to tell her something. She walked over and picked up the weapon, followed by the lyre.

"I am also skilled with a bow."

"It will be dark soon. It would be unwise to travel in the dark, alone."

"Then what should I do—stay with you?"

"If you wish. Robbers will be less likely to attack at night if there are more than one of us. Used though I am to solitude, I'd welcome a little company." He smiled again. "I've two good trout baking in my fire pit. You're welcome to share."

She found it difficult to refuse when he looked at her like that. All at once, she had a deep desire to get to know him better.

"That sounds good," she said, "I am a little hungry."

"You have a horse?" Before Terpsichore could answer, a soft whinny came from behind a clump of bushes. A pretty, creamy-gold mare, with a black mane and tail and four black stockings trotted up to her. A white star graced her forehead as she tossed back her forelock and stood with one foreleg raised. *I am Sal*.

Well, it appeared she could still speak to animals, and understand when they spoke to her. *"Hello!"* She took hold of the mare's bridle and nodded in Myrddin's direction. "Here she is. Her name's Sal."

Myrddin held out his hand and the mare stretched her neck to nuzzle him.

"A good simple name for a fine looking mare," he said. "Come then, before our supper's baked away to nothing."

~*~

At his campsite, Terpsichore unsaddled her mare and Myrddin was pleased to note the two horses soon grazed contentedly together.

While they ate the succulent fish, Myrddin studied his guest. Close up she was even more breathtaking. High, delicate cheekbones, full, coral pink lips—large sea green eyes with lashes so long and thick they cast shadows on her face.

23

Had he imagined the soft radiance surrounding her at the waterfall? It must have been an illusion, a trick of the light. She looked perfectly normal now, if 'normal' was the word for one so lovely. She was surely hiding something from him, though. Why had she not given him her family name? It had not escaped his attention that she had told him he could 'call' her Cora, and not that it was actually her name.

He noticed she ate very delicately, although she appeared to enjoy her meal. He tried to contain his own hunger and to eat a little more slowly. He did not want to give the impression he was a ruffian—not that she looked the type who was easily perturbed and she'd already indicated she was capable of taking care of herself. He somehow felt he wanted to give her a good impression of himself, though. He sighed. What was he thinking? What did it matter what impression he gave her? She would most likely be leaving the next day, and anyway, he should not be thinking of any woman other than Gwendolyn. Certainly, he should not be thinking the kind of thoughts that crept into his mind every time he looked at Cora.

When they'd washed down the fish with clear, cool water from the spring, the sun dipped below the horizon. Soon *Arianhod*, the moon goddess, rose full and majestic, from behind the mountains. For a while, they sat before the fire in companionable silence.

"So tell me," Myrddin repeated at length, "is your home very far from here?"

She gave an almost imperceptible shake of her head. "It won't take me long to get there, I'll leave at dawn tomorrow." She eyed him with a curious expression in her eyes. "Where are you journeying to, if I may ask, and have you come far?"

"North, to Castell Madog, another day's ride from here. I have been travelling for five days and nights. My journey is nearly over."

She did not ask, but something about the way she looked at him compelled him to add, "I'm on a quest to rescue the Lady Gwendolyn, who has been abducted from her father's home by Madog."

"I see—there is a reward for her return?"

Myrddin pursed his lips, annoyed she should think his motives so shallow. But they hardly knew each other, why would she have any reason to believe otherwise?

"No, this is a matter beyond mere riches. She is my betrothed."

He thought a flicker of a shadow crossed her face, but in an instant it was gone.

"Oh. And do you love her?"

"As I said, we are betrothed, and have been since we were children."

"That does not answer my question."

Myrddin was not sure whether to be irritated or impressed by her directness and lack of guile. "Of course. Why should I not love her? She is the fairest of all maidens, and the most pure—that is—" He realized he might inadvertently have insulted his beautiful companion. "Forgive me, I did not mean to suggest—"

She laughed softly, a laugh like of water tinkling over pebbles. "Don't worry; I understand what you're saying."

"And you?" he asked in turn, "What are you doing alone and away from home?"

She hesitated a moment. The brat slipped down around her shoulders. The firelight shone on her hair and turned it to flame.

"I...I had a task to do here, given me by my brother. Now it is completed and I can return."

"Are you quite sure you'll be all right alone? Perhaps I could go some of the way with you?"

"No, thank you, there is no need. I wouldn't think of asking you to go out of your way, I will be in no danger, I assure you."

Myrddin nodded and poked the fire a little more. "We should get some sleep so we can leave early tomorrow." He walked over to where he'd stashed his saddle. He placed it on the ground near the fire, for a pillow, laying his brat down as a blanket. He glanced across to where Cora was doing the same. "Will you be comfortable and warm enough for the night?"

She laughed again. "I'm sure I will. It's hardly a chill night."

"That's true." He watched as she lay down and wrapped the copious folds of her own brat around her. The faint scent of honeysuckle hung in the air, a fragrance that seemed to be part of her. This woman disturbed him and he was not sure why. He knew there was something she kept back from him, but then, he had not told her everything about himself, either. Nothing happened without reason and he could not rid himself of the feeling that their being thrown together was no coincidence.

Chapter 4

Terpsichore lay still, pretending to sleep. She covertly watched Myrddin, who sat by the fire, his brat wrapped round his shoulders. It seemed he could not sleep, either.

So, he had a lover, a woman to whom he was betrothed. Curiosity made her reach out to his mind, to try to read his thoughts, although part of her rejected the idea of such an intrusion. His mind was not open to her, however, and much as she felt intrigued to know his real feelings for Gwendolyn, it might be just as well. She was not certain if she really wanted to know. It was strange, though, perhaps she had been away from Olympus too long. Apollo warned her that her powers might wane. Perhaps, also, she had partaken of too much mortal food and was in need of ambrosia.

When he first told her of Gwendolyn, her heart sank and a pain seized her very being. Why should his state of betrothal matter to her? Surely she was not attracted to this man—a mortal?

Long ago, she made a promise to herself never to fall in love with anyone who was not immortal, like herself. The thought of loving someone for a few, brief years and then losing him when he made his inevitable journey to the underworld was more than she could bear.

But, oh, he had such an air about him. Something that called to her like no man ever had.

If only she were able to ask Apollo's advice, or even her father's. She'd tried to call to Apollo but she could not reach him, any more than she could enter Myrddin's mind.

It seemed her task here was not completed, after all, otherwise, why would she have been given the means of travelling with Myrddin? Or could it merely be Apollo's way of getting her out of a difficult situation? It might have been tricky to explain why she wandered these mountains, with no horse and only a knife for a weapon, if Sal and the bow had not appeared so fortuitously.

That must be it. For, if she thought with her head, instead of letting her heart run away with her, what reason could Apollo or her father have for wanting her to travel with this stranger? She would sleep now, and return to Olympus at first light, as soon as she'd said farewell to Myrddin and seen him on his way. Then she could forget him. But something told her, however hard she tried, even on Olympus, she would never forget those blue eyes and the way they looked at her.

~*~

28

The glowing red sparks appeared a few hours before dawn. Terpsichore looked across to where she could just make out Myrddin, lying close to the fire, apparently asleep. She stood and wrapped her brat around her shoulders. What unearthly lights were these? In the name of Hades, she had never seen anything like this before. She watched them as they advanced and retreated, advanced and retreated. They seemed to beckon to her. She walked forward a few steps. This was not natural. She sensed evil, but of a kind she had never come across before.

She tried to turn her head, to look away and move back to the fire. Some force compelled her to keep staring at them, to move forward. Further and further from the campfire she wandered. The air grew chill and she pulled her brat more closely around her. The flickering lights gyrated in a wild dance, inviting her to follow them. Dawn was approaching. In the dim early morning light, she could make out demon faces, red glowing eyes, hands outstretched, with flames at their fingertips.

She recoiled in horror. Somewhere in her subconscious, she knew she was in deadly danger, but still she moved forward. They summoned her to follow and she could not help but obey. She tried to call to Apollo, and her father, but her mind was numb. She could reach no one on Olympus.

"Myrddin!" No sound came from her lips. Still, a strange unearthly power obliged her to walk forward toward those eerie, mesmerizing points of light.

The ground grew soft beneath her feet. Cold mud oozed between her bare toes. The further she walked, the deeper the mud became; eventually, she realized she was up to her waist in chill, muddy water, and she was powerless to turn back, or even

to move any more.

"Zeus, oh, Father, please help me...don't desert me now."

For the first time in her eternal life, she knew fear. These creatures of nameless evil had her trapped. They would drag her down to the underworld and she would never see Olympus or her family again.

Then strong arms encircled her, swung her round.

"Cora, look at me." She gazed into two pools of azure blue, filled with concern, and a pale face set in resolve. Still she had an irresistible urge to look at those weird, flickering lights. She turned her head, and at the same moment, there was a flash like lightning. The ground behind her burst into a wall of blue flame. It blotted out everything, engulfing the demon lights and the hideous forms that a moment before had lured her onward.

"Look at me. Look at me...don't look back again."

Before she could reply, he swept her up and carried her back toward the campfire.

Eos in her chariot had started her journey across the sky and the pearly light showed their camp and the two horses grazing nearby. Never had anything looked so welcome. Never had Terpsichore felt so safe in a man's arms.

He set her down, near the fire, and wrapped his own brat around her. He wore only his truis, and was bare-chested. "You're trembling, you'll catch your death of cold...but that would be better than the fate which almost befell you."

Her eyes brimmed with tears as she gazed up at him. Neither her tears nor her trembling had anything do with her recent encounter. Being so close to him unnerved her even more than the fiendish, fiery lights. The thought of his protective arms around her, just a few moments ago, sent searing heat through her veins. There could be no point in trying to deny it any longer. Despite her vow, she'd fallen in love with this mortal. She loved him more than she'd ever loved any man, or any god, either. She looked at his slim body, firm and athletic without being too muscular, golden hairs sprinkling his broad chest, and she ached to touch him.

Slowly she stood, and placing her hands on his shoulders, pressed her face against him for comfort, inhaling his cool, masculine scent. It reminded her of pine and musk and warm evenings with the tang of the sea. The feel of his bare skin against her face did things to her over which, goddess or not, she had no control.

Once more, his arms enfolded her. She felt the touch of his lips against her hair.

"You're safe now, Cora. I won't let anything happen to you."

He mistook her longing, her desire, for fear. Could he not feel the beating of her heart, or did he put that down to fright as well? She took a deep breath. She was a goddess. She would not be seen to be weak and frail, like a mortal woman.

She drew back from him a little, and gazed up into his eyes. "I know, and I thank you for...saving...me from..."

The words stuck in her throat as she once again lost herself in his eyes. His face wore such a gentle expression, so much concern in his eyes. His lips were so close to hers.

"From what, Cora? Did you know they were the *Ellylldan*? Do you realize how much danger you were in?" He brushed the hair from her face with the back of his hand.

At his touch, fire coursed through her body. Terpsichore held her breath and pressed even closer to him. Clasping her hands around his neck, she hungrily drew his mouth down to hers. As he returned her kiss, she parted her lips and his tongue first teased, then slid between them and caressed her own. He deepened the kiss until she felt delirious with the ecstasy of it. Her heart thudded so hard it was almost painful. This man would drive her to madness. Did mortal women feel like this?

She tingled from head to foot, and a sweet ache throbbed deep within her. She molded her body to his, her breasts burning against his bare chest. Never before had she felt this way when a man kissed her...never had she wanted any man so much. Never had she felt so nearly mortal. She felt his arousal, and closed her eyes in surrender. Then she heard his faint, ragged intake of breath as he ceased the kiss and released her.

Gently, he removed her hands from around his neck, holding them in both of his.

"I'm sorry, Cora. This is wrong."

If someone had slid a knife between her ribs the pain could not have been more intense. She closed her eyes, not wanting him to see the hurt in them.

"You know I am betrothed," he went on. "Forgive me. It was just...I was so relieved the Ellylldan didn't take you."

"Take me where? And who are the Ellylldan?"

"Goblin fire." He dropped her hands, put an arm lightly around her shoulder, and led her back to the campfire. He poked it with a stick until it flared up and she drew closer to the heat. "The Ellylldan lure the unwary into the bog land. Those who follow them are never seen again." He paused. "Of course, you are not from these parts, so you would not have heard of them."

"I had the sense of evil...an evil older than time itself."

Myrddin nodded. "They are certainly an ancient evil...and not confined to Cymru either. They appear in different guises in all four corners of the world."

Terpsichore wondered how he knew so much. It seemed, however, there was a lot about Myrddin she did not know. She wrinkled her nose as the heat from the fire dried the mud on her clothes, producing a putrid smell. "I think I should bathe and get rid of this mud."

"I'll clear up here while you're away."

Terpsichore held out his brat. "Thank you for this. I'll be fine now."

"You're sure you're not cold?"

She nodded.

Myrddin took the garment from her and draped it over his own shoulder. "Don't stray out of earshot...but you'll be safe from the Ellylldan now, it's almost full daylight."

"I know. I'll only be at the falls. Don't worry about me."

On the pretext of removing a clean set of clothing from her saddlebags, Terpsichore walked over to where the horses grazed on the rich grass.

"Goodbye Sal, I wish we could have been together longer." She rubbed the mare's head and planted a soft kiss on her muzzle, then walked toward the falls without looking back.

Once at the pool, she removed her soiled garments and stepped into the clear water. She walked beneath the waterfall and reveled in the feeling as it cleansed the black, encrusted mud from her body. The sense of euphoria she'd had the last time she bathed here did not return. She still felt at one with the spring, but even that could not ease the ache deep inside her. It would break her heart to leave, especially without saying goodbye to Myrddin, but it was better this way.

He was obviously devoted to Gwendolyn. She must resign herself to the idea that he would never give himself to another woman as long as Gwendolyn still drew breath. True, he'd kissed her, long and hard, although it was she who instigated the kiss. She sighed. He was a man, and she knew men enough to understand few would refuse the kiss of a beautiful woman. She had no false modesty about herself. But she had few illusions, either. Despite her own feelings, she would have thought less of him if he'd forsaken his betrothed.

Terpsichore bathed swiftly. The sooner she returned to Olympus, the better. She would not stay here to yearn for someone whose heart belonged to another. Perhaps Apollo could heal the torment she endured. She left the water, dried herself, and was about to don her customary chiton when she heard the call of a raptor high above. She lifted her head to gaze into the bright sky, now clear and blue with the fullness of day.

A magnificent goshawk circled gracefully above her...a hawk, Apollo's messenger. As she watched, it swooped earthward to land on an old tree stump a short distance away.

"Terpsichore, do not return home yet; go with Myrddin, he is in great danger, although he does not know it."

"What sort of danger—and how can I help? I inspire men to dance, not to fight."

"I cannot tell you more. You will know soon enough, when the time comes. There is more at stake than one man's life. Be watchful. Above all, make sure he stays in this land. He must not cross the sea." The bird flapped its great wings and took to the skies.

Terpsichore shaded her face with her hand and watched until it became a tiny speck and then disappeared from sight.

Well, what was she meant to make of that?

Apollo could prophesy the future—a gift she and her sisters shared, to some extent. But why had he not told her the whole of it and why could she not see it for herself? She remembered the Musagetes had warned her she might lose the ability of foretelling. Was her mind so clouded by love she could see nothing else, or had Zeus simply deprived her of the gift for reasons of his own?

She sighed. If circumstances were different, she might be tempted to go against her brother's wishes and return to Olympus in defiance. She'd completed her assignment. Did she not have the right to go home? She could not deny, however, that she would relish more of Myrddin's companionship, despite her previous resolve. No, she would go with Myrddin, keep him safe, until he and Gwendolyn were reunited. However much it hurt to see him with another woman, if danger threatened, how could she desert him?

From empty air, she produced a tunic and truis, similar to those worn by Myrddin. A léine was not the most practical of garments to wear when riding a horse, and she suspected she might be in the saddle for some time.

Chapter 5

Myrddin tightened his saddle and looked over his shoulder as he heard soft footsteps behind him.

"You're back. I wondered if I would see you again."

She seemed surprised, almost startled. "I didn't think I'd been so long. Besides, how far did you think I'd have travelled without my horse?" Her tone seemed unusually sharp. Perhaps she'd been more upset by her experience with the *Ellylldan* than she let on.

"That's a good point, I don't suppose you'd want to leave such a good animal behind. I have saddled her for you, the girths just need tightening."

"Thank you. You are very kind." She pulled the leather strap up a couple of holes and vaulted into the saddle before Myrddin could offer assistance.

Perhaps it was for the best. After the incident before she went to bathe, it would probably be wise to have as little physical contact as possible. The kiss had disturbed him more than he cared to admit—not that he hadn't enjoyed it. The opposite, in fact, he'd enjoyed it far too much. He should not even be thinking of another woman, no matter how intriguing and beautiful she was. How could he have been so disloyal to Gwendolyn? What must she be enduring as Madog's captive? She would be so frightened, and here was he, allowing a beautiful stranger to seduce him, while his future wife faced who knew what perils.

"Where did you say your home was?" How many times had he asked Cora that question, and how many times had she avoided giving him a direct answer?

"I didn't, but I'm travelling north, too." He knew she lied. Why? Why could she not trust him with the truth?

"Indeed. Then it would seem pointless to travel alone."

"If you can keep up with me."

He barely had time to mount Harri before Cora sped off at a gallop. *Come on Harri, are you going to let her beat you?* Harri stretched his neck and took off after her. The mare was fast but Harri would catch her. Damn the woman. She could ride all right, but at this rate, the horses would be exhausted before noon.

~*~

38

They made good time. Sal proved to have as much stamina as she had speed and Cora was equally tireless. Any private worries he may have harbored that she might slow him down soon disappeared. He would have enjoyed the companionship of such a beautiful and accomplished young woman, but there was a barrier between them now. She seemed cool towards him and he could only assume it was because she, too, regretted that kiss.

They needed to slow down considerably in order to traverse the tortuous path over the mountains. After a brief stop to rest and water the horses and consume a meager lunch, they rode through a thick forest. The light was fading fast when they reached the edge of the forest. An area of flat grassland spread out before them, and Madog's hill-fort rose in the distance, on the summit of a steep slope. "How far is your home from here?" Myrddin asked, as Cora drew the mare alongside Harri.

"Why do you ask?"

"I would like to see you safe before I fight Madog for the return of my betrothed."

"You needn't worry about me. I have my knife and my bow. I am well able to look after myself. Besides, I'm coming with you. You'll need someone at your back."

There was such determination in those dark green eyes, Myrddin almost laughed.

"Oh, you think I'm the one who needs looking after?"

"Probably. I owe you a favor. You saved me from the Ellylldan. I'll not let you fight alone."

The tilt of her chin told him it would be useless to argue with her.

"Don't tell me because I'm a woman I don't know how to fight. I expect I'm better trained in the use of a bow than you are."

"I don't doubt it," Myrddin replied, trying not to smile. Almost unconsciously, he put his hand on the light sword at his side. "We'll need to leave the horses here and approach the fort by stealth. I don't know how many guards Madog has posted. He must surely know I will come for Gwendolyn."

"Then it's even more important you don't go alone." She gave him a quizzical look. "How do you intend to overcome a fort full of armed men? Madog's not going to make it easy for you is he?"

"I have a few means of defense he knows nothing about. Don't worry, this mission is not as foolhardy as you may suppose."

They dismounted and loosened the saddles, leaving the horses to graze. Under cover of the deepening dusk, they crept toward the silent citadel, crawling on their stomachs to avoid anyone spotting them. It took a long time to cross the grassy expanse and by the time they reached the base of the hill, darkness had fallen.

"At least we're not so likely to be spotted by the guards," Myrddin whispered. "Stay close to me."

The route to the top was steep and the going difficult. Myrddin avoided anything that seemed remotely like a path, relying on his instinct, and his ability to see in the dark, like a cat. From time to time, he glanced behind him to make sure Cora was all right. To his relief, she obeyed him and stayed close, so close in fact, he feared that if he slipped, he would take her with him. Every few minutes he'd turn and whisper to her to keep still, while he listened for signs of movement above, or any indication their presence might have been noticed.

Somewhat to his surprise, they made it to the top without incident. The tang of salt hung heavy in the air and the crashing of waves on the Western side came to them on the wind.

They approached the deep, encircling ditch. Two men guarded the single bridge. Myrddin rendered them both unconscious and Cora dealt with another who jumped out of the darkness when they reached the gate in the palisade beyond.

Once inside the boundary wall, they hunched down and worked their way toward where, if this fort was built along similar lines to other similar structures, there should be a small side entrance to the inner courtyard. They were almost halfway around when three forms appeared out of the shadows. As the moon appeared from behind scudding clouds, he saw three huge dogs crouched, ready to leap. All three snarled, showing sharp, wicked teeth, their eyes glowing red.

Myrddin tried to contact them with his mind, but the first one sprang at him before his thoughts could reach it, almost knocking him off his feet. His fingers gripped the hilt of his knife. They were mere animals, acting on instinct, and he hated to kill them, but he would not risk either his own life, or Cora's.

"No!" Cora hissed the muffled exclamation as she rushed in front of him, pushing his knife-hand aside and causing him almost to drop the weapon. The dog recoiled and leapt again, this time knocking Cora to the ground. The other two dogs dived in like a pack of wolves, downing their prey. Horrified, Myrddin drew his sword, but even as he raised it to strike, all three dogs backed away and sat quietly. Cora stood, bent down and fondled each of the dogs in turn.

"They'll be all right now, I didn't want you to hurt them; they were only doing their job." Myrddin shook his head in bewilderment. He grabbed hold of her arms and swung her around to face him. "Are you hurt? That was a foolish thing to do, you might have been killed."

Cora brushed the dirt from her clothes. "Well, I wasn't, I understand animals. I knew I could get through to them without them hurting me, I'm fine"

"We'd better get on before we're spotted." Myrddin breathed a silent sigh of relief. He understood animals himself, but doubted if he could have subdued the dogs so easily. He appreciated Cora's affection for animals and her respect for life; it mirrored his own. In that instance, though, he'd been afraid she was hurt and his only thought had been to protect her. It seemed she had no need of his protection, however. She wasn't fooling when she said she was capable of taking care of herself.

At last, they found the small gate that led into the main courtyard of the fort. With caution, they moved along the wall, which enclosed a circular area of grass, cobbled in the centre. Myrddin heard a slight sound from above, and reached for his bow from the baldric slung across his back. He fired and was rewarded by a muffled thud; then came the hiss of another arrow. A further thud followed almost immediately, as a heavy body hit the ground close to the first. He glanced at Cora and she looked at him with a grin of satisfaction on her lovely face as she slung her own bow back on her shoulder.

"Your distaste for killing doesn't extend to people then," he whispered, as they continued around the wall keeping their eyes open for more guards.

"I aimed for his shoulder. He didn't have all that far to fall, the ramparts are low. The most he should suffer is a few broken bones."

"Well, that's all right, then," he said, unable to keep a note of sarcasm from his voice, "I'd hate for our enemies to be badly injured. Follow me. We need to find a way into the main structure."

After crossing the courtyard to the central building, they spotted two guards each side of a large, wooden door.

"Can you arrange a distraction?"

"Of course."

Before he had chance to caution her, she slipped into the moonlight. In a soft voice, she began to sing, removing her brat and swirling it around her head. She moved her hips in the rhythmic way she had the day he first saw her and danced as if no one was watching.

Both guards stood as if mesmerized. Myrddin crept behind them, grabbed hold of each of them and banged their heads together. The next moment, they both lay unconscious on the ground.

Cora was by his side again, in an instant. "Fine," she said, studying the structure, which was obviously bolted and barred on the inside, "but how do we get in?"

"Like this." Myrddin touched the door with the pommel of his sword, muttered a few words in a low voice, and it swung open. He noted the expression of surprise on Cora's face, but there was no time to stop and explain. Myrddin half expected there would be guards on the other side of the door. However, a glance at the heavy bolts, chains and bars that secured it assured him that under normal circumstances there would be no need for guards. He made some signs in the air and spoke the necessary words; the door swung noiselessly shut.

He beckoned Cora to follow him along a short corridor. They found themselves in a hall, dimly lit by torches in iron sconces high up on the walls. Deep shadows leapt out at them, making it difficult to see clearly. Myrddin looked around. The hall appeared deserted. With some caution, they crossed it and went through an archway at the far end. The left- hand side of the corridor in which they now stood was in darkness, the right-hand one was illuminated by flickering torch light. From behind a closed door halfway along, they heard the sound of girlish laughter.

"Gwendolyn!" Myrddin exclaimed under his breath.

The next moment, he heard a slight sound behind them and turned to see an armed guard. He struck with his sword but as he went down, the man yelled a warning. Before Myrddin had chance to use his sword again, or draw on his magick for defense, the door burst open revealing another half-dozen armed men, swords raised. They surrounded Myrddin and Cora and although Myrddin prepared himself to fight to the death, he knew they were hopelessly outnumbered.

Chapter 6

"What is the meaning of this?"

In the flickering light, cast by the myriad candles in their iron holders suspended from the ceiling, stood a man, legs apart, sword raised. Not quite as tall as Myrddin, but of imposing stature, thicker set and of muscular build. He commanded respect, armed or not. His fair hair was long and wavy and his beard neatly trimmed. A young woman, richly clad in deep blue velvet, with long golden curls down to her waist, sidled up to him and put her hand on his arm.

He indicated his men should stand back, although Terpsichore noted they did not lower their swords, and he kept his hand on his own.

She glanced at Myrddin. Although he wielded his own sword at the ready, his attention seemed riveted not on the man before them, presumably the abductor, Madog. Rather, his gaze rested on the girl. This must be the beautiful Gwendolyn, Myrddin's betrothed. She could understand why he would be smitten with her, although she found it disconcerting he should prefer a mortal woman over a goddess. But then, he did appear to have a very strong sense of loyalty, and she had to admit, Gwendolyn was as fair as any mortal woman she'd ever seen.

Myrddin seemed to draw his gaze from Gwendolyn with an effort.

"Myrddin ab Morfryn, what reason do you have for entering my fortress by stealth, like a thief in the night?" the bearded man demanded. "I could order you killed, and your companion with you."

"We have come to rescue Gwendolyn, who, as you well know, is my betrothed."

Myrddin's sword was still drawn, but Terpsichore noticed he did not seem in any hurry to use it. His face wore a perplexed expression as if matters were beginning to make sense to him and he was not happy about it.

Something like a smile played about Madog's lips although Terpsichore noticed his fingers tightened their grip on his own sword.

"So you think you can just invade my fortress and take the woman I love—"

"Myrddin, be gone. Can't you see, I am in no need of rescue," Gwendolyn interrupted haughtily. Her eyes blazed, green as the grass on the brightest summer's day. Her porcelain cheeks flushed a deep pink, to rival the petals of the roses in her hair.

Madog gazed at her with a fond expression on his face. "She is right. Put your weapons away. Gwendolyn is free to leave at any time—if she so wishes."

"But I do not wish," she interrupted, stamping her foot and glaring at Terpsichore and Myrddin. "I am staying here, with you, my lord." She turned and looked at him, with adoration in her eyes. Myrddin replaced his sword in its scabbard, and Madog followed suit, although the two men did not take their eyes off each other. Terpsichore also sheathed her knife, and glancing at Myrddin, noted the frown of consternation on his face, although his eyes were expressionless and she could glean nothing fom his mind.

"And how did you propose to 'rescue' Gwendolyn, supposing you had been able to infiltrate my fortress without being apprehended. I suppose you intended to kill me?"

"If I had to," Myrddin replied in a heavy voice. "Although, you should know, killing is not my way, unless there is no alternative."

"Perhaps," Madog said, "we can discuss this matter without the need for bloodshed. I will overlook the rudeness of your arrival, since you appear to labor under a misapprehension."

He stood aside for them to enter the room and indicated one of the many comfortable couches, while he and Gwendolyn took another..

"Please be seated.Would you like to introduce us to your lady?"

Myrddin glanced at Terpsichore. "This is Cora, but she is not my lady. As you know full well, I am betrothed to the maiden who sits at your side, Gwendolyn. The woman you abducted."

Gwendolyn leapt up. "That's a lie!"

Madog beckoned her to sit again and leveled his gaze on Myrddin.

"And what makes you believe she was abducted?"

Terpsichore might not be able to read Myrddin's thoughts, nevertheless she sensed the confusion and doubt in his mind.

"Gwendolyn's father beseeched me to rescue her. He led me to believe she was taken by force."

"The old man is a fool and a liar," Madog retorted. "Gwendolyn and I have known each other all our lives. Despite the bargain made between your families when you were children, we grew to love each other, although Gwendolyn's father never liked me. When he refused to ask you to release her from your contract of betrothal, she ran away to be with me."

Myrddin looked directly at Gwendolyn. "Is what Madog says true, do you really love him?"

"Yes, Myrddin. It is, and I do. I could never marry you—I hardly even know you."

A grim little smile played about Myrddin's mouth. "That much, at least, is the truth." He rose to his feet. "Madog, it appears I have misjudged you. I allowed myself to be deceived into going on a fool's errand. Deal with me as you will—but please, I ask you to let Cora leave unharmed. She is merely a travelling companion and has no part in any of this."

Madog also stood. "Myrddin ab Morfryn, few have been our dealings with each other, but many are the tales of your deeds. They say you are wise beyond your years, a strong ally and a formidable foe. Killing you would serve no purpose and I would prefer you were my friend rather than my enemy."

Myrddin inclined his head. "Then you have both my friendship and my allegiance. I see you are a man of honor. If ever you have need of me you have but to ask."

The two men clasped hands. Neither smiled, but Terpsichore was aware the tension had lifted.

"We should leave," Myrddin said. "It is late."

"Indeed it is," Madog said, "but you must stay the night. You know yourself it's not safe to travel in the dark in these parts. You can leave at dawn tomorrow."

Terpsichore rose as Myrddin thanked their host. Things had not turned out so badly after all. News that Gwendolyn was in love with Madog must have come as something of a shock to him, though.

She sighed. It seemed Myrddin was not the only one sent on a fool's errand. The danger had not been so great. For once, Apollo's foresight was wrong. Myrddin would doubtless have been fine, without the assistance of a muse. A muse whose presence he scarcely seemed to notice.

A serving wench escorted her and Myrddin to their separate bedchambers. A fire blazed in the hearth and the bed was comfortable. She found it difficult to sleep, however. She kept her knife under her pillow, and when sleep eventually came, her dreams were all dark and of a man in the shadows, wearing a brazen helm.

~*~

Thanking their host, they left the castle early the next morning after a hearty, warming breakfast. Once across the bridge that spanned the ditch, they made their way down the hillock by the main path. The route was a great deal easier than the one they took the night before. In less than an hour, they reached the grassland. It did not take quite so long to reach the area where they'd left the horses.

They found them grazing beneath the trees. Terpsichore checked her saddle. Her lyre was still safely secured, as she'd left it. She rarely went anywhere without her lyre, it was almost an extension of herself. However, it would have been a little impractical to carry with them the previous evening.

They mounted, and rode back the way they'd come. Terpsichore turned and looked behind her. She could not rid herself of the feeling all was not as well as it seemed. She felt a presence, another immortal, and he was not far away.

They entered the shadowy forest. Myrddin watched Cora's straight back as she rode the golden mare along the narrow track between the trees. A shaft of sunlight filtered through the branches above them, striking her beautiful hair and causing it to gleam with the luster of a burnished chestnut. They'd barely exchanged a word since leaving Madog's fort. She seemed deep in contemplation, or perhaps she was still angry with him over that kiss.

He could not bring himself to regret it, especially now, since he need have no more loyalty to Gwendolyn. Was that all it had been then? Loyalty? He'd believed it was love, but now, he knew Gwendolyn had never cared for him, the emptiness and sorrow that should have descended over him was strangely lacking. In fact, the sensation he felt was more one of relief. He shook his head. The realization gradually dawning on him was something he should not even contemplate. He urged Harri on a little and drew up alongside Cora. At least he could try to settle things between them, to attempt to rekindle whatever friendship they had, and hope to earn her forgiveness.

She looked across at him, and those ocean green eyes were devoid of emotion.

"You're angry with me," he said. "I apologize if I have offended you."

"No, I'm not offended, or angry. Why should you think that?" She hesitated. "I'm sorry about Gwendolyn. It must have come as a shock to know she went with Madog willingly."

He smiled slowly. "A surprise, certainly. Her father indicated she was taken by force. Now I suppose I'll have to return to him and tell him his daughter has a mind of her own and is perfectly happy." He was not sure if he should believe Cora when she denied being angry. Something must be causing her to avoid his glance, and to have ridden so far in silence.

He paused. He knew he shouldn't ask. He risked offending her again, but he couldn't help it. He needed to know.

"Where are you really from?"

She gave him a look of injured innocence. "What do you mean, where am I really from?"

"You implied you were from the North, and we were both headed in the same direction. You didn't carry on Northward when we left the fort, though."

Now he'd started he might as well carry on. "You've never actually told me where your home is."

She returned his gaze this time, and smiled, the faintest of smiles that seemed to light up her exquisite features. "I understand your curiosity, but I think you've a few secrets of your own."

He tried to conceal a start of surprise. What did she guess?

"Why do you say that?" he asked with narrowed eyes.

"The way you opened the door to Madog's fortress. And before that, the wall of blue flame when I was threatened by the Ellylldan. It wasn't natural. There was sorcery involved."

What did she know of sorcery? Was she some sort of enchantress? Certainly, he found himself falling more under her spell with each moment. "You mean it wasn't you?" he queried making the question sound innocent.

"No, you know it wasn't. I was mesmerized by the creatures, I couldn't—" she stopped short, and he smiled, a mirthless smile as she fell neatly into his trap.

"You couldn't use your own sorcery because you were under the spell of the Ellylldan, Myrddin finished for her. So she *was* an enchantress. But he needed to hear it from her. He did not believe she had knowledge of the dark arts, unless he was fooling himself, believing what he wanted—what he needed—to believe. So who was she?

"Tell me the truth. You are not a witch, I would know if you were. But you talk to animals and move like no one I've ever seen. I think you are no ordinary woman."

"No more than you are any ordinary man."

They stared at each other in silence for a moment.

"I am who I say I am," Myrddin said at last. I've not tried to deceive you in any way. It is true, though. I have some small...power, a certain skill in manipulating the natural forces, a communion with nature."

She watched him astutely. "I guessed as much. You don't have the air of a common soldier, even if you dress like one. Apart from a little sorcery, I know you, too, can talk to the animals"

"And you, who are you really...*what* are you?"

"You wouldn't believe me if I told you."

The track levelled out and without another word, she urged Sal into a canter and drew away from him. Myrddin had no choice but to follow. What did she mean—he wouldn't believe her? He'd seen enough wonders in his life, he was aware that, given faith, almost anything was possible. Including the knowledge that whoever or whatever she was, she aroused feelings in him no other woman ever had. The flame she'd ignited when he first saw her had grown out of control and become a raging inferno.

He needed her...he loved her.

Chapter 7

They drew rein before they reached the edge of the forest. Ahead of them, lay the steep mountain trail. Myrddin swung Harri round to face Terpsichore who now rode abreast of him.

"Why have we stopped?" she asked.

"The horses should rest before going further.

The trail through the mountains is difficult, even though the return journey is downhill." He waved to a little brook, which meandered through the trees. "There's a stream here where they can drink. Also, I think we need to talk."

There was an edge to his voice and she guessed he was upset about Gwendolyn. Did he still believe he loved her? The woman had made it obvious she felt nothing for him. Was he so blind? Could he not see how much better off he'd be with her, Terpsichore...a goddess? Someone at least his equal?

She frowned. Of course, he didn't know she was a goddess, but that was hardly the point. On the other hand, why should she expect him to stop loving Gwendolyn just because his love was not returned? Knowing he loved another did nothing to dampen her own passion, if anything it made her long for him even more.

"Couldn't we talk while we ride?" Terpsichore was not sure why, but she wanted to get as far away as possible. She could not shake off the sense of approaching danger.

"I think not." Myrddin dismounted, and with a sigh, Terpsichore followed suit. She removed Sal's saddle and bridle, seeing him do the same for Harri. The grass beneath the trees grew rich and green. The horses would not stray far and she knew she could call them back if necessary.

"You said I wouldn't believe you if you told me who you were. It would be nice to have the chance."

She gave a shrug of resignation. Those azure eyes fixed on her with a steadfast expression, which made it clear he would not rest until he had an answer.

"Very well." She drew herself up to her full height and tried keep her voice steady, although it was difficult when he looked at her like that. "I am Terpsichore. I'm a muse...of the dance, to be exact."

For a long moment, he did not reply. Then he nodded his head slowly. "I believe you," he said, "but I'm not sure I understand."

"I'm a muse," she repeated. "A goddess of inspiration. I'm responsible for the feeling you get when you hear music and can't keep your feet still. When your spirits lift and all your cares and worries seem as naught; that is me, in your mind. It's not the first time I've visited this land you call Cymru. I returned because your people were so busy defending the land, they forgot how to dance."

She paused, aware Myrddin was gazing at her in rapt concentration. "You may think it a frivolous thing, but when people forget how to dance, and to make music, the heart goes out of them and they also forget how to live. My sister, Euterpe, came here long ago and instilled a passion for music and song, which remains. But my brother, Apollo, knew they'd lost the memory of how to use it, how to express in their dancing, the sheer joy of living. So I returned."

"And have you given us back our love of dancing, then?"

She was not entirely sure if he was making fun of her.

"Indeed, I have, don't you feel it in your soul?"

"I might, if you were to show me again how you dance."

Now she was sure he mocked her. "You don't believe me, do you?"

There was no doubting the sincerity in his eyes as he said quietly, "Yes, Terpsichore, I do. I could watch you dance forever. My soul could use some uplifting. Will you dance for me, now?"

He reminded her so much of her brother. Oh dear, Apollo! He'd told her not to reveal her true identity. But then this man was different. He was far more than just an ordinary mortal. Well, if she had to shed her pretence—and since she couldn't really get into the mood of the dance wearing truis— an instant later she was dressed in her customary chiton, a garland of flowers in her hair.

57

Slowly she moved, singing her accompaniment in a low voice. Soon, she lost herself in her dance, almost forgetting Myrddin watched her. Her arms raised above her head, she moved her hands in rhythm with her feet, All the while, swivelling her hips as she turned in small circles. She raised her voice a little and became aware of Myrddin softly singing with her. It was no surprise when he joined in her dance, as well. No one could stand still for long when she played her lyre or danced. Wasn't that her task anyway, to fill all mortals with the sheer pleasure of dancing? Wherever she danced, in taverns or market places, everyone forgot what they were doing at that moment, to join in. Myrddin, it seemed, was no different. If only she could control her heart as well as she did Myrddin's feet. If only she could control *his* heart.

"You dance well...for a 'warrior'."

He smiled, causing her heart to flip once more. He was so incredibly good looking when he smiled.

"Thank you, but I've never pretended to be a soldier, although I can fight if need be. I wear these clothes because they are more practical for riding." He chuckled softly. "And I was taught some refinements as a boy. Not your sort of dancing though. I've never seen anyone dance like you."

"I can dance any way you want me to."

"The way you dance now is perfect, but perhaps we could try dancing together?"

She caught her breath. Had he any inkling how she felt? Was he deliberately trying to make things even more difficult for her?

He stood just behind her and a little to the side. Slipping his arm around her waist, he took her left hand in his, with her right hand in his own right one. Of course, she knew this way too, but it was unnerving to be so close to him, to have his hands touching hers. Somehow, she managed to keep singing, to make her feet move in time to the tune.

"Are you sure you're not still angry with me," he asked again after a while, bending his head a little, his breath caressing her cheek, his face so close to hers she almost stopped breathing herself.

She ceased singing and stood still. As one, they let go of each other's hands and stood, the uneasiness between them returning.

"No, I told you. What makes you say that?"

"You've spoken very little to me, since the night of the Ellylldan. I assumed you were annoyed—or at least displeased—with me."

"I admit I was not very happy that you kissed me and your thoughts immediately turned to Gwendolyn. It wasn't very flattering."

"So that's it. You *were* angry with me."

She stood back a little and tried to look at his face without giving her feelings away.

"I wasn't. I just...no, I wasn't angry. Why should I be? You were to have been married. I knew that. I should not have let you kiss me. If I'm angry with anyone it's myself." It did not escape her notice he was gallant enough not to point out that, in fact, it was she who kissed him. "It must be hard to love someone and then find they love someone else." *Oh, no one knew better than she, how hard it was.*

"A blow to my pride, certainly."

"And not your heart? You're telling me you were willing to marry a woman who meant nothing to you?"

Myrddin sighed. "Not exactly. It was a marriage arranged by our father when we were still children. We only met a few times; we didn't really know each other. Gwendolyn was right about that. But...she is very beautiful and I thought I loved her. I really did."

Terpsichore wished more than ever she still had the power to read thoughts. The possibility he might no longer care for Gwendolyn, and be free to love her, was torture. Yet, did she really want to love a man who fell out of love so easily?

"I'm trying to understand. Are you saying you no longer love her, even though came all this way and risked your life to rescue her."

"It was my duty. She is...was my betrothed. Her father is not only a fool, he's devious, too. He had me believing she'd been abducted. By her own admission, that's not the case, and she ran away, to be with Madog. I didn't know that at the time, of course, and it would have brought dishonor to her and to myself to refuse to rescue her. She, however, obviously has no such scruples about keeping her word." He frowned. Those blue eyes were very earnest when they gazed into hers, with an expression that implied he was anxious for her to understand. "Would you believe me if I said I was relieved when Gwendolyn said she loved Madog?"

Relieved? He was relieved, yet he'd told her he'd loved his future wife. She needed to be sure.

"So you're saying ...you don't...love her?"

"I realize I never really loved her. I did not know what love, true love, could be, until now."

He looked at her with such a grave expression on his face she could hardly bear it.

"You see, what I felt for her was nothing compared to what I feel for a certain beautiful goddess, who claims she is the muse of dance."

Terpsichore stood close to him again and looked steadily into his eyes. They held sincerity and a gentleness she'd seen in few men's eyes before.

"Then...then you love me?" she whispered, trembling like a mortal woman in the throes of first love.

"I do Cora...Terpsichore. More than words could ever tell you. You're a goddess, and far above me, I know. Still, I cannot help how I feel."

She placed her arms around his neck, and gazed up at him. "But we hardly know each other either. How can you be sure?"

"I think you're laughing at me, Cora. There is such a thing as love at first sight. I felt it the first time I saw you. I didn't want to believe it I hoped it was a passing infatuation, that I could stay true to Gwendolyn, but...she never set my blood on fire."

"And I do?" She couldn't help it. She had to tease him a little; he'd kept her waiting long enough.

"Let me show you." He pressed his lips against hers. Holding her face in both his hands, he kissed her softly. Then he parted her lips with his tongue, and kissed her with even more passion than that first time, after he'd saved her from the fire trolls.

She pressed closer to him, feeling her body responding to his, with a need she could not, and did not wish to control.

"I love you, with all my heart and soul, more than life itself." He whispered, holding her even tighter. The warmth of his body seemed to set her blood on fire and her heart pounded.

"And I you, Myrddin ab Morfryn." The flimsy chiton was no barrier against his touch, and when his fingers caressed her breasts her whole body burned with longing like the flames of Hades itself. Never had she felt like this before. Never had a man aroused such feelings in her.

With a gentle movement, he removed the garland from her hair, and she shook her head; her hair cascaded round her like a cloud. He kissed her neck and throat—sliding his lips down under the loose folds of the chiton. His long fingers slipped the garment off one shoulder and his lips fastened on her breast. His tongue circled and teased until she gasped, so great was her yearning for him.

He lifted her in his arms and carried her to the shelter of a massive oak tree. Beneath its spreading branches, he tenderly laid her on the grassy floor, then knelt and held her against his chest. She could have removed her chiton the same way she'd donned it, but it was more fun to have him do it, although her need cried out to him to hurry. She performed the same service for him, but the truis were somewhat tricky and she used a little magick for haste. They lay together warm skin to warm skin, heartbeat to heartbeat. Terpsichore ran her fingers over his firm, slim body in awe. She hadn't expected him to be so...perfect. His lips met hers again and as he covered her body with his own, she raised her hips and arched her back to meet him. She slipped her hands around his neck, ran her fingers through his hair and pulled him even closer, delirious with desire and the need to be one with him.

They rose and fell together, like the waves upon the shore below the citadel they'd so recently left. She hardly heard the words of love he whispered; her spirit soared in the sky with the Horai, flying with Apollo's hawk. As her soul melded with his in the rapture of their joint climax, wave upon wave of ecstasy thrilled through her body. Their minds, too, became as one. She knew for certain, then, that he possessed magick no mere mortal knew. He'd communed with forces older than the Earth itself.

He was mage!

Chapter 8

Terpsichore lay back on the soft carpet of grass and blossoms, beneath the sheltering oak. Her head rested against Myrddin's chest, his arm cradled her shoulders. She gazed at the cloudless sky and sighed in contentment. How long had they lain here? They'd made love until, exhausted, they dozed in each other's arms. She never wanted to move from this place. She wanted to stay wrapped in his embrace forever. Her mind sang with the knowledge only now acquired. He was a mage...and he loved her. She raised herself up on one elbow as he stirred.

At the same time, she thought she heard a woman giggling, and a drunken hiccup or two. She listened intently, but all was silent save the cheeping of the birds. It must be her imagination.

Myrddin's blue gaze regarded her with the adoration worthy of a goddess.

"We should leave," she said, "We've slept a little. I don't think it was for long, but even so, we should go now."

He sat upright, with not a trace of drowsiness. "Why, my love? There is no hurry, or is it that you are anxious to return to your home?"

She shook her head. "No, I'm not sure I even want to return home...now I have you."

"Why then are you so anxious to leave?"

"I'm not sure. I...I feel we're in danger. Or at least, you're in danger. I've felt a presence ever since we left Madog's fortress. I can't explain it. Don't you...sense anything?"

Myrddin shook his head, "No, and I normally know if there is danger nearby. Are you sure you're not imagining it?" He raised an eyebrow as if he wondered if a goddess was even capable of imagining such things.

"I can't be certain," she admitted. Perhaps." She wondered, for a fleeting moment if Dionysus were near by, taking a perverse delight in watching them make love. She recalled the tell-tale hiccups, that waft of laughter sensed a few moments ago. But Dionysus was not known for his stealth, surely she would have heard him and his entourage sooner, probably smelt his wine as well. Perhaps Myrddin was right and it was all in her imagination.

"Well, if you think we should leave, we will."

Myrddin was on his feet and reaching down, he pulled her to him and kissed her once more—a soft, adoring kiss that lingered on her lips.

She luxuriated in his closeness and the warmth of his body for a moment, before she once more donned her inar and truis. It took Myrddin only a minute or two to clothe himself, then they called the horses, and swiftly saddled them and remounted.

The mountain path was not long, but it was steep and narrow, with many sharp turns. It took all their concentration, riding single file and watching where the horses trod.

"So where are we going?" she asked, when eventually they reached the bottom and urged the horses into a brisk trot.

Myrddin closed his fingers on the reins and looked across at her. "We seem to be headed back in the direction we came. There's nowhere in particular I need to be. How about you? You never did tell me where your home is."

"Don't you have a home then, or family?" she asked, avoiding his question.

"No, I have no family, no home. I am a wanderer."

A rush of compassion filled her heart. She thought of her own family, her stern but loving father Zeus, and her beloved mother, Mnemosyne; her dear sister muses, and her many half sisters and brothers. To have no home, no family, how could he bear it?

"I will be your family now. I will give you love...children."

He slowed Harri back to a walk as he looked at her. His face wore an expression of infinite sadness. "But you have your own home and family to go to. They must be wondering where you are...even if you are a goddess." He smiled softly, "Don't worry about me. The love we've shared will last me all my life. I'm used to being alone, to live the life of a wanderer. I may even leave this land and, cross the water—"

"No!"

Myrddin again raised his eyebrow in that querying gesture she found so compelling.

"I have no reason to stay. I thought of leaving when I realized Gwendolyn and I were not meant to be. You will return to your family and there will be nothing to hold me here." He reached across and took her hand. "I know enough of the gods to realize your dwelling place is not of my world. I know I cannot enter with you, I am mortal"

"But you are a mage. You are not like ordinary men."

He smiled slowly, a wistful expression in his eyes. "I am still a mortal. Your world is not mine, I wish it could be otherwise."

Terpsichore read the sorrow in his eyes, as if her ability to enter minds was restored. She knew beyond doubt his heart would break, as would hers, if they had to part.

Tears filled her eyes and she reached for his hand and gripped it in hers. To have found love, only to lose it so soon. What had she done to displease the other gods so much they could play this cruel trick on her? She squared her shoulders in determination. There had to be a way.

"Promise me you will not cross the sea."

Myrddin did not answer.

"Promise me."

"If it pleases you, my love, I promise."

"Thank you. I will ask my father to help us," she said, her voice low and heavy with emotion. "It would not be the first time a mortal loved a god and was allowed to enter Olympus and live among us..."

A glimmer of hope flickered across his face. Before he could answer, however, the blue sky turned black, and then glowed with a lurid orange tinge, like the flames of a distant forest fire. A wind sprang up from nowhere and whipped the branches of the trees. Some would have believed it a summer storm. Terpsichore knew otherwise, glancing at Myrddin's face she realized he knew it was not a natural force as well. Fear gripped her heart.

"Run, my love," she yelled above the howl of the wind, "Run!" Terpsichore leaned forward over Sal's neck, and the animal leapt into a swift gallop.

Harri needed no urging to take off after her.

Myrddin risked a quick look over his shoulder. In the sky, a quadriga, drawn by four horses snorting fire, bore down on them. He dropped the reins, standing up in his stirrups and turning, in an archer's stance. This was no earthly enemy.

His hand strayed to the bow slung in its baldric across his shoulder. Perhaps he could kill the charioteer with an arrow. Immediately, he realized this was unlikely, for he flew high above them. Myrddin was an expert bowman but his arrows would not reach that far, even though their pursuer was drawing ever closer. If only there were some way to stop him. Terpsichore, he must protect her. He concentrated his mind. A wave of water rose, higher than the trees. At the same time, a narrow chasm opened up before them. The two horses leapt simultaneously to land, safe, on the other side. As they galloped on, Myrddin looked back again. The chariot and horses burst through the torrent of water, the jets of fire from the horses' nostrils caused it to vaporize with a fierce hissing sound.

"What enchantment did you use?" Cora asked, turning her head toward him as they sped onwards. "Never mind," she said, the wind whipping her words back to her. "Nothing will stop Ares, he's closing in on us."

Myrddin risked another look back. The chariot had touched the earth on their side of the chasm. He caught the glint of gold on the horses' bridles, the charioteer standing tall and dark, the sun's rays striking his bronze helmet and breastplate.

"Ares?"

"The god of war!"

"What? Why is he after us?"

"He isn't...not *us*...he's after *you*."

~*~

Terpsichore felt the powerful muscles of the horse beneath her, the pounding of hooves filling her ears as they sped over the ground. How long could they keep this up? Sal, she knew, had supernatural stamina and strength. Myrddin's Harri was immensely powerful but he was still a mortal horse. They could not outrun Ares. What did he want with Myrddin anyway? She had no quarrel with her half-brother, herself. It had to be Myrddin he was after, although she could not imagine why.

She remembered the flash of bronze glimpsed in the halls of Olympus the day Apollo asked her to return to Wales. It was Ares spying on them. Of course, she should have guessed. It still did not explain the reason for his pursuit. The black and the golden horse raced neck and neck. She glanced behind her. Ares was close. The clouds of dust churned up by his quadriga mingled with the smoke and fire from the nostrils of his four mighty horses, Aithon, Phlogios, Konabos and Phobos. Her eyes stung and the smell of burning dust made it difficult to breathe. She reached for her bow and turned in the saddle as Myrddin had. Shoot her own brother? Yes, if she had to. As Ares raised his spear toward Myrddin's back, she took aim.

At the same instant, Myrddin wheeled Harri round. "Cora, watch out!" His hand was on his own bow, but he never loosed the arrow. Terpsichore's aim was true, she hit Ares where she'd intended, in the shoulder, and deflected the direction of his spear...instead of piercing Myrddin through the heart it hit him higher up, in the chest, near the shoulder. With a sharp cry, he slipped from the saddle. Terpsichore drew Sal to a halt and threw herself to the ground beside Myrddin's motionless body.

Seizing the spear, she drew it out and flung it from her.

Tears spilled from her eyes. The tears of a goddess. Even they could not save him. The bright blood stained his tunic, spreading across the cloth. Gently, she turned his face to her and kissed his brow. His eyes were closed, his skin deadly white. By

Hades, her aim had not been good enough, had not stayed Ares' arm sufficient to prevent a grievous wound. Oh Myrddin, why did you turn?

He had feared for her and in so doing exposed himself to Ares' fury. In her heart, she knew it would have made no difference. Ares would have struck Myrddin with his spear even if he'd fled for his life leaving her, something she knew he could never have done.

She turned to the tall, darkly handsome warrior clad in brazen armour. His four stallions stood nearby and pawed the ground with their hooves. Ares struck fear into most mortals, but Terpsichore was a goddess. She felt only contempt for her brother, the god of war and destruction.

"Why, Ares, why?" she demanded, her voice trembling with grief. "What did I ever do to you that you could break my heart by murdering the man I love?"

With an almost casual air, Ares removed the arrow from his shoulder and broke the offending shaft in half. The wound seemed to trouble him little, although he scowled as he threw down the two pieces.

"Well, sister, I knew not you would give your heart to this frail mortal, or that you would shoot your own dear brother in his defense. I have my reasons for wanting him dead."

"But...why...what reasons? What good is his death to you?"

In her anguish, the only thought in Terpsichore's mind was Myrddin, his lifeblood seeping into the rich Welsh soil. She held him closer, as if she could sustain his wavering life-force.

Ares threw back his dark head and laughed. He bent his handsome face close to hers.

71

"Because, Terpsichore, he would have instructed the one who is yet to come. He would have instilled in him the ways of peace, to wage war only in order to prevent it. I cannot allow that." He laughed again, a sound to chill the blood. "Do you really still not know who your lover is?"

Terpsichore turned from him, icy fingers clutching at her heart. It mattered not who Myrddin was. All she wanted was to save him, whatever the cost.

Apollo, Apollo, my brother, where are you when I need you? Her soul screamed in anguish and despair. Never had she felt so alone, so forsaken. Never had such grief filled her whole being with the pain of it. Tears spilled down her cheeks, her body wracked with sobs.

"Hush, sister, hush. He is sorely injured but he knows you love him. You showed him what happiness was, nothing can ever destroy that." A gentle arm slipped around her shoulder and she looked up into the beautiful purple eyes of her sister, the muse of tragedy.

"Melpomene! I should have known I could rely on you to comfort me at such a time. Oh, Melpomene, how could this happen?"

"Tragedy happens all the time, dearest Terpsichore, as its muse, I can only do what I can to ease the pain." Her voice was gentle, her hands soothing, but still Terpsichore felt no comfort. From the corner of her eye, she saw a quick movement. She turned her head to see Ares perilously close, brandishing his sword.

"Step aside; I want to finish the deed, to make sure he does not live to—"

"No, Ares!" Terpsichore flung herself across Myrddin's still form. She flung her arms around him to protect him. "You will have to destroy me, too!"

"Desist, Ares. At once!" A mighty clap of thunder announced the arrival of Zeus himself. The skies grew black and bolts of lightning flashed as the earth shook. Even Ares would not disobey the might of his father. He moved away and knelt before him, although his dark eyes blazed defiance.

Terpsichore drew back from Myrddin, one hand still laid upon his arm, but she too knelt in deference to the mighty Zeus. She threw Ares a look of pure hatred. Raising her head, she perceived Zeus's face, dark against the whiteness of his beard, his brow furrowed in anger.

He pointed an accusing finger at Ares who ducked as lightning bolts sped past him.

"What is the meaning of this? You dare to seek to murder a mortal outside the confines of battle? Think not that you will go unpunished."

Terpsichore looked at Zeus appealingly. "Father, where is Apollo? There may yet be time to save this man whom I love."

"Yes," Zeus said, his voice losing its sharp edge. "However, Apollo seems to be elsewhere just now." He gave a mighty bellow and the wind lashed the trees, thunderclaps echoed from the mountains and lightning streaked the sky. "Dionysus!"

"You called, oh mighty, Zeus?"

Oh, Hades. Was her whole family here? Everyone it seemed, except Apollo.

She looked at the wine-sozzled god, with his ubiquitous following of maenads

He glanced at the scene before him and looked at Terpsichore with an expression bordering on compassion.

"Do you know of Apollo's whereabouts?" Zeus bellowed.

Dionysus gulped and shook his head. "Perhaps he has gone to Delphi...his oracle—"

"Think well before you answer, Dionysus. Protecting your brother will only serve to lower you in my estimation and make me vexed." He lowered his voice to a roar. "And you know what happens when I am vexed!"

Terpsichore almost felt sorry for Dionysus, torn as he seemed to be between loyalty to Apollo and fear of his father. She knew well that Dionysus was beloved of Zeus, but that did not put him beyond his wrath.

"I believe...that is...er I believe he had an assignation with Aphrodite."

"Whaa-at?" Again, lightning lit the skies and thunder crashed around them. "And where, pray, is he holding this 'assignation'?"

"I don't know," Dionysus whimpered. "Really, I don't."

"Then you had better use what powers your drunken spirit can summon and find him," Zeus commanded. "Don't come back without him— and take your harlots with you!"

Terpsichore turned back to Myrddin. There was little time to waste. He might not survive until Dionysus returned. "I will give him anemos..."

"No, my daughter, that will not be enough to save him, not when with a wound as grievous as this, and made by Ares' spear. I would give him anemos myself, but my power is too strong, it would kill him."

With sudden resolve, she straightened up. Still with Melpomene's arm around her shoulder, she looked her formidable father in the eyes. "Then I will visit the moirai and bargain with them for his life."

Zeus studied her from under his shaggy brows and shook his head. The white hair swirled like a storm around his shoulders, almost dislodging his wreath of oak leaves.

"Daughter, you know there is no bargaining with the fates. I tell you this as the *moiragetes*."

"Perhaps, Father, but I must try. If there is the slightest chance of saving him I must do it."

Zeus frowned. He seemed to ponder for a considerable time and Terpsichore wondered if he was ever going to speak. Or was he so angry at her temerity, he chose to ignore her?

"You are either very brave, or very foolhardy, my daughter. However, although on the point of death, he still lives. There may be a way, if you can find it." His usually fierce face softened as he regarded her with a compassion she did not often see in her stern father. "Go then, Terpsichore, before I change my mind and forbid you. But take care the moirai do not trick you. You know where to find them—and I will request the Horae to leave the way open for you."

"Thank you, Father." She stood and inclined her head in respect, gave her beloved sister a swift embrace, and letting light envelop her, returned to Olympus.

Chapter 9

Terpsichore's mind raced with many thoughts and questions. She still did not understand why Ares tried to kill Myrddin...had nearly succeeded. Why did her father not seem surprised by her being with Myrddin? And where was Apollo?

Once through the great gate of clouds, she thanked the Horae, and then crossed the square courtyard, at the southern end of Olympus. She made for the quarters of her father and Hera, her stepmother. Hurrying past the kitchens and servants' quarters, the kennels, stables and chariot houses, she reached the doors of the grand Council Hall where Zeus held Court. Flinging them wide, she strode inside. Ranged on each side of the Hall were five magnificent thrones, one for each of the principle Olympian gods. Terpsichore stole a look at Apollo's; empty, as she knew it would be. Where was he? How could he desert her when she needed him so desperately? She remembered his words when he gave her this assignment, so long ago it seemed now. *I may not be able to help you.* Had he foreseen this? Was she being punished for something she didn't know she'd done?

Hera and Zeus's thrones stood side by side facing the open courtyard. When the doors were open, they could see the surrounding firmament, and if they wished, watch the mortals go about their business below. Zeus's throne was unoccupied as well. Of course, he was still with Myrddin. Did that mean Myrddin lived? He must. He must. How could she go on if she lost him? Hera, Zeus's wife, her stepmother, was most likely in the living quarters she shared with the King of Olympus. Her ivory and gold throne, with its crystal steps held no presence.

It came as no surprise to her that beautiful Aphrodite was missing, too. She looked around. Those gods who remained surrounded themselves with mists of invisibility, although she could vaguely see their forms. She approached Zeus's black marble throne with some trepidation. The moirai demanded respect from all, and their fellow gods were no exception. Only Zeus, the moiragetes, leader of the fates, was not in awe of them, and even he held them in great esteem. Were they not given the greatest honor and allowed to sit nearest to his throne, closer than even his daughters, the muses?

Seven steps led to the throne, each one a different color of the rainbow. An eagle of gold, with ruby eyes sat on the right arm. Zeus's purple ram's fleece, used by him to provide rain in times of drought, lay on the cold and empty seat.

She peered into the shadows at the side of the throne. They were there. Klotho, the youngest, fair hair piled on top of her head, spun the thread of life. Lakhesis, middle-aged but still comely, measured the thread with her rod, and decreed the quality of each life. The most fearsome of all, the ancient Atropos, cut the thread with her shears. Each snip meant a mortal met his death. Terpsichore drew a deep breath. *Please. Let me not be too late, let his thread be still uncut.*

Atropos looked up, sheers poised. "'Tis one of the young muses, Terpsichore. If you come seeking Zeus, you are too late. He is not here."

"Thank you, I know he's not. It's the three of you I wish to speak to."

Something like a cackle escaped the old crone's lips. "Indeed? It is rare for anyone to come looking for us, especially the muse of dance. Would you not be better inspiring mortals instead of bothering us at our labor?"

"Oh, let her speak, Mother," Lakhesis broke in, not for an instant taking her eyes off the thread she measured. "Terpsichore, what do you want with us child?"

Terpsichore drew herself to her full height. She would not allow Atropos to intimidate her. "I wish to ask a favor. I am willing to pay."

"Pray, what have you that would be of value to us?" Atropos interrupted.

"What—what would you wish me to give?" Terpsichore asked, realizing she trod dangerous ground. She shrugged inwardly. No matter. She would give anything, even her immortality, if only Myrddin could live.

"Be gone, girl. Surely you know no one—not even your father himself—bargains with the fates."

"What is it you would have of us?" The question spoken in quiet tones was from Klotho, who up until this moment had remained silent.

"There is a man. A mortal. Myrddin ab Morfryn—he has been sorely wounded by Ares' spear. I ask that he may live."

"I was there at his birth," Klotho said softly. "I spin the thread of his life. I would see you dance, I am in need of some entertainment. There should be more to existence than spinning. Dance for me."

Atropos 'tutted' over her shears, but Terpsichore bowed in compliance and began to dance. This was easier than she'd anticipated, although the last thing she would have done from choice was dance.

Dancing and the delight and inspiration of the dance were her life, her very existence. But she found it difficult to sing or to dance with her spirit so weighted down with grief. However, as she moved and glided before the fates, she became captivated by her own movements and lost herself in the rhythm. Not for a moment did she forget Myrddin, however, and the usual joy and spring was absent from her steps, although she hoped this was not apparent to her watchers.

At last, she slowed and spread her arms to signify the end of the dance. Klotho signalled her to keep moving and before Terpsichore realized her intention, the moira joined her in the dance, leaving Atropos to do both the measuring and cutting while Lakhesis took over the spinning.

Atropos's humor did not seem to be improved by this arrangement but Terpsichore had little option other than to continue with the dance.

Klotho had more grace and energy than Terpsichore would have supposed and whirled to the song the muse sang, her white robes swirling around her. The day had been exhausting enough and even a goddess wearies. Was Klotho ever going to tire? On, and on and on they danced. Just when Terpsichore feared the dance might last forever, and Myrddin would never be saved, Klotho came to a halt and took her place beside Atropos and Lakhesis.

Terpsichore caught her breath. "Well," she asked, "will you save my love's life...let him live?"

Klotho shook her head and stared in concentration at her bobbin as she eased the un-spun thread from the distaff and resumed her spinning. "No, I'm sorry, I can't help you."

"But you said..."

"I said I'd like you to dance for us. I made no promises. I only spin. Ask Lakhesis; she measures the length of the thread."

Terpsichore turned to the woman who sat between Clotho and Atropos.

"What would you ask of me to set my lover free from the threat that hangs over him?"

"What would you give?" Lakhesis asked in return.

"Anything you ask, if it's in my power to give," Terpsichore said. She looked her in the eyes and tried to appear more at ease than she felt. The moirai had a way of draining the confidence from even a muse.

Lakhesis reached out and took hold of a strand of Terpsichore's pride and joy—her hair, glossy, thick and wavy—and long, oh so very long.

"Brides leave us locks of their hair as offerings. What about you—would you be willing to give us your hair?"

"If it would save his life," Terpsichore whispered, "then yes."

Lakhesis made to take the shears from Atropos, but Terpsichore sprang back, pulling her hair from her grasp. She remembered her father's parting words. She might be about to make one of the greatest sacrifices in her power but that did not mean she had to trust them. This was especially true of anything concerning Atropos's deadly shears.

"I'll do it," she said firmly. She took her knife from her belt. The blade was sharp. She shook out a hank of her hair, half the total thickness, which was all she could hold in one hand. With the other, she sliced cleanly across, just beneath her ears, and the shimmering dark red-brown locks fell to the marble floor. She did the same with the rest and watched Lakhesis gather up the silky strands and fondle them with evident glee and satisfaction.

"Now will you give me back his life?"

Lakhesis smirked in a self-satisfied kind of way. "My poor muse, it was never mine to give. I merely measure the thread. Atropos is the one who cuts it and ends a mortal existence."

Terpsichore felt her cheeks burn with anger although she did her best to hide it. Despite her father's warning she'd allowed herself to be tricked. However, it was best not to show her feelings to the moirai, even Zeus withheld his fury from them.

"There seems little point in trying to bargain with you any more," she said as calmly as she could. "You are playing games with me. It's clear you never had any intention of granting my request."

"You mean you no longer care what happens to your lover?" The old hag's voice crackled like dried leaves underfoot and her pale grey eyes, usually lifeless and dull, glowed with spite. "Then be gone muse, and leave us to get on with our work."

Terpsichore had never felt such complete and utter despair as descended on her now. Whatever it took—whatever it cost her—while there was a chance, however slight, that Myrddin might live, she had to take it.

"If I pay what you ask, will you give me your word you will not take his life?"

Atropos waved her shears in the air. "You have my word I will not cut the thread of his life."

"Nor allow Klotho or Lakhesis to do so?"

"Don't risk vexing me, Muse. You've tried my patience long enough. No, they will not end his life, either. Now how much is he worth to you? Would you give me your immortal soul?"

Terpsichore drew in her breath. To give up not only her godly immortality, but her soul. To be enslaved forever to the whims and demands of these three. She thought of Myrddin, his gentleness of spirit and his inner strength. The powers she'd not known he possessed. His face, so fine and so pale as his lifeblood drained away. "Yes," she said at length. "Yes, I will do that if it will save his life."

To her amazement, Atropos threw back her head and let out a hideous cackling laugh. "You are made foolish by love, muse. Of what use is your soul to us? We are not Hades or Ares, we do not deal in souls."

She paused. "There is something, though."

Terpsichore was torn between relief and trepidation. "Oh," she said, in a loud, clear voice, hiding her emotion. "What would that be?"

"Why, anemos, of course."

Of course! What else would the old crone— Terpsichore hastily corrected herself, shielding her thoughts—the old lady want from her? Her essence, her life-force energy, or some of it anyway. It was a long time since she needed to bargain this way, and she knew it would take a hundred years to restore anemos, once given. No matter, Myrddin was worth the sacrifice, she would willingly give some of her anemos, if it meant he would go on living. She would have given it to Myrddin directly, if by doing so she could have saved his life.

"I accept," she said and stepped toward Atropos.

Immediately the old woman stood and placed her bony hands on her shoulders. Terpsichore gasped. A shock ran through her and her whole body seemed to shudder and to turn cold for a moment. It was as if all the breath were sucked out of her. A greenish-white light shone between them, then everything went dark.

Chapter Ten

"Lie still, daughter, don't move for a while."

"Mother?"

"Yes, Terpsichore, now lie still. It will take time for you to regain your strength."

Terpsichore tried to rise but fell back into Mnemosyne's arms.

"I told you to lie still. You cannot give anemos and expect to be on your feet at once."

Her mother soothed Terpsichore's brow with her hand. "Your hair," she murmured, your beautiful hair, you were so proud of it."

The mist that filled Terpsichore's head gradually cleared. "It doesn't matter," she managed to whisper. "It will grow again." She opened her eyes and discerned the three moirai seated by Zeus's throne.

"M—Myrddin," she gasped, "H—have you spared him?"

To her dismay, Atropos broke once more into peals of high-pitched laughter, joined by the two younger moirai.

"Foolish child, he was never in danger of dying. His thread of life is never-ending."

Terpsichore's mind clouded once more. Had she heard aright? You...you mean he's immortal, too?"

"Did I say that?"

"Then what?"

"Do not ask foolish questions. All will become clear in time."

Terpsichore turned to her mother and again tried to rise. "I have to get back, Mother. Myrddin. I love him so. But of course...you don't know—"

"But I do, naturally. I know all about this Celtic mage of yours."

"Then...then you know I must go back to him, he may not die but he is sorely injured, and Apollo was not to be found."

All at once, the marble walls of the Olympian halls shook. In a blaze of glorious light, Zeus strode up the hall toward his throne. He stopped and gazed down at her, and she saw kindness in his eyes, not the annoyance she'd half expected.

"So, daughter, you love this man enough to not only give anemos, but to offer your immortal soul. Do you know what you would have given up if your sacrifice had been accepted?"

Terpsichore nodded weakly. "Yes, Father, I do, and I would have given my immortality willingly to save him." She lowered her gaze. "Can you understand a love like that?"

He smiled, the crows' feet at the corners of his eyes appearing even deeper, like canyons and valleys in a desert landscape. "You may find it hard to believe, Terpsichore, but as a matter of fact, I can. Although, my anger would have been

86

boundless had you indeed renounced your immortality." He rolled his eyes. "You are not the first of your sisters to fall in love with a mortal and sadly, I don't suppose you will be the last."

"Father, how is he? I must go to him."

"Do as your mother says and rest for a while. He is in good hands. Apollo is with him."

"Apollo? Then he has returned, praise be." Tears of relief filled her eyes. "I must go back to him."

"Yes, you should return...when you are stronger. You must make the most of what time you have left with him."

Mnemosyne's voice held a note of unease. "Are you sure you'll be all right? Your aura's very faint..."

"Dearest Mother, I'm fine." Terpsichore rose to her feet, and was obliged to hang onto the folds of Mnemosyne's chiton for a moment to avoid falling to her knees.

"I said you were still weak. Rest here for a while longer. Take some ambrosia..."

"No, Mother, I'm all right, really. "I just want to go back to him."

"You will take some ambrosia first," Mnemosyne said in the tone of voice Terpsichore knew meant she would tolerate no argument. "You will be no good to this Celtic mage of yours if you are weak from hunger as well as the transfer of anemos."

"Do as your mother says and partake of some sustenance," Zeus growled, before she could argue the point.

With an air of resignation, Terpsichore took the bowls of ambrosia and nectar Zeus drew from the air and laid before her. After only a few mouthfuls, to her relief, she felt the life flowing back into her, the ambrosia and nectar strengthening her life-force, renewing her immortality. When she finished, she perceived her aura glowed again, weaker than before, but nevertheless, discernable.

Bidding Zeus farewell and with one last kiss from her mother, she walked back over the courtyard to the cloud gates, where the horai waited.

The words of her father came back to her. "Make the most of what time you have left..."

What had he meant by that? She'd been too drained of anemos to question it at the time. Surely Zeus would have told her if all were not well with Myrddin. Could it be that Apollo had been unable to heal him fully after all? No, it was not possible that the god of light should fail. Perhaps Zeus meant Myrddin was not immortal, and compared to that of a muse, his lifespan was the mere blink of an eye. Whatever the truth of his words, she knew she would not be at ease until she was back once more in the arms of the man she loved.

~*~

The pain faded and Myrddin fell into the void, a black abyss of nothingness with no way out. How long he floated, helpless in this state between life and death he had no idea. When at last he opened his eyes, he hastily closed them again. The golden- haired man kneeling beside him was not only young and incredibly handsome, but he glowed. A light emanated from him, similar to the one he had seen surrounding Cora—Terpsichore—when she was not aware he watched her. The light from this man though, was even more brilliant, like the rays of the sun.

He turned his head a little and beheld a beautiful young woman with long red hair and amazing violet eyes. He tried to rise, searching for the one face he wanted to see.

"Terpsichore, where is she?"

The young man withdrew a short distance and the woman came closer. She also glowed, but not as brightly as the man.

"Lay still, Myrddin, you must rest."

"But where is she—and who are you?"

"I am Melpomene, Terpsichore's sister. That is my brother, Apollo, he healed you."

Myrddin glanced down at his léine, stiff with dried blood. All at once, he remembered fleeing from Ares, fear for Cora filling his mind. He recalled turning to make sure she was still safe...then a burning pain in his chest. That was his last recollection, after which...nothing. He shook his head. He'd come up against a number of supernatural creatures but Greek gods were something entirely new to him. The pain had left him and he felt no weakness.

He glanced around again, thankful to note not only that there was no sign of Ares or his fire breathing horses, but that Harri stood nearby, safe and unharmed.

"Where is Terpsichore?" he asked once more. A chill like the ice of deepest winter crept through his veins, a sense of loss descended on him. If she had left...if he were never to see her again—

Melpomene laid a gentle hand on his arm.

"Don't distress yourself. She will return. When you were injured, Apollo was...elsewhere. Terpsichore was so afraid for you she returned to Olympus to bargain for your life with the moirai."

"The moirai? Who are they?"

"The fates, they who determine the lifespan of all, be they mortal or god."

"But surely the gods are immortal...?"

"We can still be killed, by accident or the wrath of another."

Myrddin rose to his feet. "Is she in danger? I must find her..."

Melpomene fixed her violet gaze on him and he felt her calming vibes wash over him.

"She may be in danger, I can't lie to you, but she is, after all, a goddess. She can take care of herself. You cannot go where she is."

Myrddin leant against the trunk of a nearby oak tree. If Terpsichore was in danger, he should be with her. If anything happened to her, how could he go on? He did not want to live without her.

"So she is risking herself for me." He glared at Melpomene, "This isn't right. Why did you let her go?"

Again Melpomene touched his arm and her soothing spirit calmed him once more.

"I could not have stopped her if I wished. Once my sister's mind is set on something—" She paused. "That's why I stayed here, so I could comfort you when you regained your senses and found her gone. You are doubtless worrying needlessly. She may not yet know Apollo has returned to heal you."

He could not help thinking that was little consolation.

"Myrddin," Melpomene said, her voice soft and persuasive, "do you think I would not know if something dire had befallen my sister."

Myrddin gave her as much of a smile as he was able, by way of thanks. She was right. These Olympians counted the ability to read minds among their other powers. He believed, he too, would know if anything had happened to Cora, but oh, how he longed to hold her again in his embrace. How he yearned to smell again the sweet scent of honeysuckle that surrounded her.

All at once, Melpomene stiffened, as if listening.

"My father has reached Olympus," she told him. Terpsichore is safe."

"Is she well?" Something in Melpomene's face made his mind cloud with fear for his beloved.

"She is weak...but...she returns."

The sky brightened. A flash of light and the clouds parted. In a swirl of mist, surrounded by the aroma of flowers, Terpsichore drifted down to Earth...and into his arms.

"Cora," he murmured, "Cora...Terpsichore, my sweet."

"Myrddin, I—I thought your wound was fatal. I thought I'd lost you." She turned her head toward Melpomene. "Sister, thank you for being here...and Apollo, too. Thank you for healing him."

91

She leant against Myrddin's chest and he felt her tremble. He kissed the top of her head and held her even closer. Her aura was fainter than it should be. What had she done?

"Cora, your hair, what happened to your hair?"

"Oh, it's of no concern, it will grow again soon enough." She gazed into his eyes as if the others were not there. "Do I look so terrible, can you still love me?"

For the first time in many hours, Myrddin laughed. "Terpsichore, my muse, you are beautiful. I love you with all my heart, with or without your long hair."

"So you sacrificed you hair and your anemos," Apollo said, "Well, at least you proved your love for him."

"There are three moirai," Melpomene said, her face troubled, "Terpsichore, tell me you didn't sacrifice any more than anemos and your hair?"

"No," Terpsichore said, looking over her shoulder, "I did not, I merely danced for them."

Myrddin gazed with awe at the woman in his arms. Anemos. She'd given anemos. If that meant what he believed it did, no wonder she was so pale, the soft rose blush to her cheeks absent. She must, indeed love him. But they were both safe and together. He needed nothing more. He would care for her; help her grow strong again.

"You are an immortal," he said softly, "but would you stay with me for my lifetime? Or is it too much that I ask of you, my love? You see, I can't bear the thought of life without you."

"I would stay with you as a mortal myself, and not count it a sacrifice," Terpsichore said softly. "But," she slipped from his embrace, and still holding on to his arm, turned to her brother. "Apollo, the moirai said Myrddin had no end to his thread of life, but he was not immortal. What did they mean? If it pleases you to answer."

"Yes, it pleases me," Apollo assured her, "in fact, I need to tell you both. Zeus and I have agreed you should know. Come, let us sit together. I will tell you of what is to be, the task Myrddin has before him."

~*~

Helios was already commencing his journey to the underworld when Apollo finished speaking. The evening sky glowed with the colors the sun god in his chariot painted, red and gold and purple.

Terpsichore gazed upon Myrddin in wonder. Now she knew he was not only a mage, but a greater one than she'd ever supposed. Although still mortal, he was as much a god as many of those on Olympus. She suspected there were still things Apollo had not told them, but he must have his reasons.

"You were destined to meet Myrddin and save him," Apollo told her. "You see now what the moirai meant."

"But I didn't save him...you healed him, my supplication to the moirai was of no avail."

"There are other ways to save a man than to prevent his death. You did everything you needed to do—and more. Even Zeus did not foresee you making the sacrifices you did to the moirai, until it was too late to stop you." He pursed his lips, but his eyes held a twinkle. "We'd originally intended you to be merely a distraction, to prevent Myrddin leaving these shores when he learned Gwendolyn loved another. We had not counted on you falling in love, or for Ares to complicate matters."

"I don't understand," Myrddin said. "Why did he want to kill me? What possible grudge could he have against me? I hadn't even heard of him until today."

"He is the god of war," Apollo said. "He represents the chaos and destruction of conflict. He must have listened in on my conversation with Zeus, before Terpsichore returned to this world, and decided to rid himself of you. He needed to stop you fulfilling your destiny, to prevent you from being the mentor of the king who is to come, of whom I have just spoken—he who will strive for justice and honor, for freedom and for fairness in battle. All the things Ares despises. Without your counsel, he would never be king. Without your assistance he will not even be born."

Myrddin looked enquiringly at Terpsichore. "How much did you already know?"

She shook her head. "Only that Ares wanted to be rid of you for the reasons Apollo just said. But that was only after he'd wounded you." She lowered her eyes to hide the sadness in them. "It seems we must part after all."

Apollo smiled. "But not yet. Stay with each other while you may. When the time comes for Myrddin to accomplish what lies before him, you will know, and for a time, Terpsichore, you must go home to Olympus."

He regarded the young man with a serious expression. "Myrddin, you will live your mortal span on Earth, as the moirai have decreed. Fear not, you will be together again, you have my word."

He turned to Melpomene, who had remained silent all this time. "Take leave of your sister, for we must return to Olympus."

The two sisters embraced, then Terpsichore bade Apollo farewell. Myrddin put his arm around his goddess, and watched with her as a cloud of white luminescence enveloped the god of light and the muse of tragedy. Then he drew Terpsichore to him and kissed her, as if he would never let her go.

~*~

Broceliande, France 585 AD

Decades came and went. The world changed. Two figures stood near an ancient hawthorn tree in the heart of a great forest.

"This is the one," the tall blond god stated, standing before the tree.

The muse nodded. Her glorious dark red-brown hair cascaded almost to her feet and her eyes shone with hope. Her lovely face showed both anticipation and anxiety.

"He will remember me?"

"Of course. If you loved each other, as you say you did, how could he forget?"

Apollo placed his hand upon the wizened trunk. A flash of light like one of Zeus's thunderbolts lit up the forest. A mighty crack echoed and reverberated. The hawthorn split asunder, the radiance now seeming to come from within. In its midst stood a still figure. After a moment, he stumbled forward from the ruins of the tree and Terpsichore saw he was old. His hair, long and unkempt, reached below his shoulders, and he carried a staff. Despite his age, there was beauty in his features.

As he drew closer, the light scintillated and within its shimmering glow he changed, straightened, grew taller. His hair darkened from white to blond and his features changed, the skin regaining the firmness and texture of youth. When the uncanny golden light faded there stood before her the young man with whom she had fallen in love, more than a hundred years before.

"Myrddin."

"Cora, oh, Cora, my love."

They fell into each other's arms, their lips meeting, melting; their kiss as passionate as the one they had first shared. It seemed they both forgot Apollo's presence. After a while, Myrddin released her, although she wanted nothing more than to stay in his arms. Taking both her hands in his, he gazed into her eyes and his own were filled with sorrow.

"Cora—Terpsichore, you are more beautiful than ever, if that is possible. My dearest one, I have been so foolish. I am not worthy of your love."

"Do not say such things." Terpsichore held him to her breast again. "It was all foreseen. You cannot cheat the fates. Clotho spins the thread and Lakhesis measures its course. Mortals and gods can but follow, even though they themselves may hold great power."

Myrddin held her close once more. "I love you more than life itself, but I must tell you. When you left me, I thought I would never look at a woman again. For a long time I contented myself with the task set before me. But then, when the king no longer needed me, when Excalibur returned to the lake, I grew lonely."

He hesitated, and when at last he went on, his voice shook with emotion. "I allowed myself to fall under the spell of the Lady Nimue and took her as my apprentice. I broke my promise to you. I left Cymru with her and traveled across the sea to this land. For a little while, she made me forget you." He hesitated again. "Then she tricked me into revealing my powers and used them against me, to trap me here. Cursed but alive, yet not living; aware of what I had lost and how much I love you, Terpsichore, but a prisoner in the dark."

"Until we set you free," Apollo's deep tones interrupted him. "As Terpsichore said, your destiny could not be changed. We foresaw what would happen, and it was meant to be." He waved a hand toward the hawthorn. "The world of mortals will believe you are still imprisoned in that tree. Many will be the legends and stories told about you. You have accomplished what you were meant to do, you mentored and guided the Once and Future King. Indeed, you were the instrument of his birth."

"And what of Arthur?" Myrddin asked. "What of my king?"

"Arthur still sleeps, for his awakening is not yet. But your work here is finished."

Apollo spread his arms wide. "Myrddin, whom future generations will know as Merlin, take the hand of your beloved and receive the reward that awaits you. Enter the realms of the immortals and live in peace and love for the rest of eternity."

Terpsichore slipped her hand in Myrddin's. Apollo placed his arms around them both. A soft wind stirred the trees. A dazzling white iridescence illuminated the landscape for a moment before darkness descended. Where the hawthorn stood before, a slender sapling grew over the remains of the old tree, and reached its branches to the heavens.

The clouds forming the gates of Olympus parted. The sweet song of the horai sounded soft and clear. The joyous melody drifted down to Earth and mingled with the voices of eight muses, singing a welcome to their sister and her one true love.

From Hywela Lyn:

Thank you for purchasing my book. I hope you enjoyed this short fantasy adventure, based on Greek mythology and some of the Welsh legends and folklore I grew up with, as well as a little of the Arthurian legends.

I love to hear from readers and can be contacted at:

HywelaLyn@hywelalyn.co.uk

If you'd like to find out about me or my futuristic adventure romance series, details can be found at:

http:www.hywelalyn.co.uk

and my Blog:

http://www.hywelalyn.blogspot.com

Made in the USA
Charleston, SC
05 November 2012